SECOND EDITION

TOUCHDOWN TOMMY SECOND EDITION

ACE COLLINS

PUBLISHING THE POSITIVE

ELK LAKE PUBLISHING INC.
Plymouth, Massachusetts

Cover and Interior Design: Derinda Babcock

Editor: Deb Haggerty

Author Represented by Hartline Literary Agency

PUBLISHED BY: Elk Lake Publishing, Inc., 35 Dogwood Dr., Plymouth, MA 02360, 2018

Library Cataloging Data

Names: Collins, Ace (Ace Collins)

Touchdown Tommy / Ace Collins

150 p. 23cm × 15cm (9in × 6 in.)

Description: Elk Lake Publishing, Inc., Plymouth, Massachusetts, 2018.

Identifiers: ISBN-13: 978-1-948888-75-2 (trade) | 978-1-948888-76-9 (POD) | 978-1-948888-77-6 (e-book.)

Key Words: Six-man football, sports, high school football, pro football, tennis, small towns, coming of age

LCCN: 2018959778 Fiction

DEDICATION

This book is dedicated to Jack Pardee, a man who came out of the six-man football ranks to become a legend in the NFL.

CHAPTER 1

"In deep formation for the Los Angeles Stars is Tommy Hillman."

More than 80,000 fans had crowded into Chicago's Mayer Stadium, and almost all of them must have heard the announcer call my name. I couldn't believe it. On this early September Sunday, I felt as though all eyes in the stadium—as well as those watching on television—were on me. Here I was, just twenty-two years old and a return specialist and wide receiver for one of America's favorite pro football franchises. I had a big red star on my helmet, a huge blue number two on my white jersey and shiny silver pants that just screamed Hollywood. I was living my initial dream. This should have been the happiest day of my life, and in a way it was, yet the announcer's voice somehow magically started a journey that took me back to another time—a time when my dream world had suddenly become a nightmare. As I thought about that day more than eight years ago, a chill ran down my spine. *Could it have been that long? It seems like just yesterday.* Yet so much had happened, and I had been so many places since that tragic time.

The referee's whistle interrupted my trip down Memory Lane and pulled me back to reality. I watched as Jim Pitts, the veteran kicker for the Chicago Firestorm, raised his hand to signal his teammates on the coverage squad that he was ready. My eyes focused in tightly on his feet as he approached the tee. Everyone, including me, held their collective breath, knowing when Pitt's toe hit the leather, the season would officially begin. And if all went well, I would be the first person to actually touch that pigskin this year.

I must have imagined the sound, the crowd was screaming much too loud for me to actually hear it, but when Pitts's foot connected with the ball, I thought it echoed like a blast from a cannon. The ball seemed to shoot off the tee and rise effortlessly toward the sky. Probably by instinct, I adjusted, took two small steps to my right and resolutely planted myself at the five-yard line as the ball flew downfield toward my position. Then, just when I was about to grab the ball out of the air, everything stopped. Suddenly, there was no crowd, no stadium, and no football. I felt as if I were standing in a fog, caught in a thick bank of white clouds rolling along the Illinois prairie. Then the clouds began to whirl, and as they did, my life literally flashed in front of my eyes at super speed. As I tried to catch up with the blurring images, as I strained to find something to latch onto to stop this wild rush, everything froze. I was still in Chicago, but things were much different. There was no game, I wasn't in a uniform, and there was no football flying through the air toward me. The only thing I heard that seemed to connect me to the previous moment was a man's voice coming over the loudspeaker. I couldn't really understand how or why, but in the split second before I was to catch the pigskin and begin my professional gridiron career, I had somehow been transported to another place and another time. I was no longer Tommy Hillman of the Los Angeles Stars, I was just another student at FDR Middle School in West Chicago.

CHAPTER 2

"Tommy Hillman. Tommy Hillman. Report to the principal's office."

As if snapping out of a dream, I found myself in the middle of algebra class, thinking more about skateboarding than numbers. *How did I get here? What is going on?* Then I again heard the droning voice.

"Tommy Hillman. Tommy Hillman. Report to the principal's office."

As Mrs. Hawkins and the entire class looked toward my seat at the back of the room, my thoughts no longer concerned how or why I was there, but what had I done? I was a good kid. I didn't cheat or copy others' work, and I certainly wasn't involved with drugs. I wouldn't think about stealing anything, either. I had never even been in a fight. So what could the principal want with me? This had to be a dream but felt so real. I was struggling to rationalize what had happened, but as the seconds ticked by, my dreams from the past became real and the reality of the present disappeared. I was suddenly back in my own past and didn't remember a thing about what had happened or *would* happen in the next few seconds, much less the next eight years.

"Tommy," Mrs. Hawkins stated firmly, "you had better hurry. You know that Mr. Rogers doesn't like to be kept waiting."

I knew *that* all right, but I was still in no hurry to get to his neighborhood. He wasn't nearly as friendly as the man in the sweater on public television. Our principal was a former Marine and was as big as a refrigerator. He was the last person I wanted to see. I always tried to avoid him in the hallways.

Knowing I had no choice, I grudgingly got up from my seat, filed past rows of snickering classmates and made my way to the hall. Walking by rows of green lockers, my steps echoed off dark and worn wooden floors. I found the office door at the end of the corridor, took a deep breath and knocked. The secretary's muffled voice instructed me to come in. As I opened the door, I noted a stern look on her face. She avoided eye contact with me as she flipped a switch on the intercom and let Mr. Rogers know that I had arrived.

"You can go in," she quietly said and pointed toward a door just beyond her desk.

I studied that door for a second, swallowed hard, and then slowly shuffled towards it. I again knocked. This time, no one told me to enter, but the large brass knob turned as if by magic, and the door slowly opened. Seconds later, a grim-looking Mr. Rogers stood in front of me, his six-foot-four-inch frame seemingly blocking everything behind him. I had never felt so small and powerless.

"Come in, Tommy," he said. As I entered, he pointed to an attractive middle-aged woman. "I think you know the school guidance counselor, Mrs. Frost."

I not only knew her, I liked her. She was one of the nicest people at school. She was always smiling, and when she talked, her voice rose and fell like a song. Yet, she wasn't smiling now, and her blue eyes weren't sparkling either. As a matter of fact, as I sat down beside her in a chair in front of Mr. Rogers' desk, those usually happy eyes seemed to stare right past me—like she didn't want to really connect. *If I did something bad enough to upset Mrs. Frost this much, I must really be in big trouble!*

Needless to say, I felt panicked. I had no idea what I had done, but the mood in the room told me that I had to be guilty. So before anyone could say anything, I blurted out, "I'm sorry for whatever it was I did. Just tell me what it was, and I won't do it again. I promise."

Mrs. Frost shook her head, then tried very hard to form words with her lips, but it seemed as though her mouth had failed her for a moment. Finally, after taking a few deep breaths, she leaned over in her chair, placed her right hand on my left and began to speak.

"Tommy," she began, her usually strong voice was cracking with emotion. "There is no easy way for me to tell you what I have to tell you. I have some bad news for you. There has been an accident."

I was still very much in the dark. I didn't have a clue as to what she was trying to say or why this accident involved me. I felt fine, and I sure hadn't seen anything happen at school that day. Suddenly, I wondered if one of my friends had been injured in a PE class. "Who's been hurt?"

"Tommy," she took a very deep breath as she continued. I waited for her to explain what she meant, but rather than clear things up, she really just repeated what she had already said. "I just don't know how to tell you this. There are no words, there is no good way." She stopped again and tried to compose herself.

As Mrs. Frost looked away from me, her eyes roamed over the principal's desk, stopping only to glance out the window at the far side of the room. As I waited for one of the two adults to say something, I somewhat relaxed in my seat. I didn't know what was going on, but if it was an accident, then I also knew I couldn't be blamed. So, I obviously wasn't in trouble. As I studied Mrs. Frost, my eyes were drawn to a picture of a football player that was hanging in the corner—an old black and white photograph of a big guy wearing a dark jersey. The player had a firm jaw, a head full of dark wavy hair, and the widest shoulders I had ever seen. Then, as if hit by a bolt of lightning, I realized the picture was of Mr. Rogers. I didn't know he'd played football—and that was a college picture. *As big as he was, he must have been good!* I was still studying the old photo when Mrs. Frost glanced back toward me, picked up a tissue, dabbed some moisture from her right eye, and continued.

"Tommy, your parents—they were in a traffic accident this morning. On the Loop. I guess they were going downtown."

"That's right," I cut in. "There was a luncheon that had something to do with Dad's business. Everyone was bringing their wives. Mom took off work. Anyway, I guess if they had some kind of wreck, it means that they are going to be late picking me up after school. That's no problem. I'll just go over to the school's courts and work on my tennis. Are they going to have to rent a car?"

Neither of the adults moved. They sat rigid in their chairs and looked at me with the most helpless expressions I had ever seen. They seemed to want to say something, but couldn't. Then I began to realize that this was not just a fender bender. There was something else going on here. Something very bad.

In the seconds that followed, as the silence seemed to scream at me, I remember a panic beginning to take control of my emotions. Suddenly my mind was whirling. *Ok, calm yourself. Things aren't that bad. People get hurt in car wrecks every day.* I then stared directly into Mrs. Frost's face, took a deep breath and asked, "How badly were they hurt? What hospital are they are in?"

She looked at me for a moment, then turned her head again toward that far window. At that point Mr. Rogers caught my attention and said in a very soft voice, "Tommy, I'm so sorry, but they ..." He didn't need to finish. I knew what the next words had to be.

Numb, suddenly feeling very alone and sick, I looked into the big man's face, a silent question hovering in the air between us. He answered with a simple, somber nod of his head.

CHAPTER 3

At first I denied it. *It can't be, no way. This has to be a mistake.* Yet, the looks on their faces told me it had happened. Staring down at the floor, I suddenly felt cold and clammy as I considered the unthinkable. *I am an orphan. Mom and Dad won't be coming home tonight. I will be there by myself. No, wait, they won't let me stay alone. I can't spend the night by myself. My nearest relatives are in Texas, what am I going to do? Where am I going to stay? What is going to happen to me?* At that moment, when things looked most bleak, I just lost it. I cried for a while, then I just sat in the chair and stared straight ahead. I think Mr. Rogers and Mrs. Frost tried to talk to me, but I don't remember what they said. Everything about those next few moments is now a complete blank—like I had died too. For the rest of that day, it seemed my life had ended, only I kept breathing and I didn't know why.

All my friends agreed my folks were the coolest adults in the whole world. I couldn't imagine life without my parents. There was so much we had planned. We were going to take a vacation to California this summer. Dad and I were going to play in a father-son doubles tennis tournament this weekend. Mom was going to take me to a soccer camp in Michigan in July. We always had dinner on Sundays at Kelps Cafeteria. Everyone knew us there, and they knew we would be there right after church. Now, none of those things were ever going to happen again. It was just like someone had taken a huge eraser and rubbed them out.

I left school before the final bell. I avoided all my friends and didn't bother picking up my books or my homework. Mrs. Frost took me to my house in her car. We found the spot where the extra key was hidden and unlocked the green front door. I halfway expected my mom to be there, that this had all be a mistake, that someone else had been in the wreck, but the house was silent—deathly silent. I was home, but all the life and warmth that had once been a part of the house, the very heartbeat of what had made this place so special, was not there anymore.

Mrs. Frost stayed with me and tried to talk to me about everything from how I felt to what music I liked. I didn't answer. I just sat on the couch and stared out the picture window without really seeing anything.

The two of us weren't alone long. As the news spread, several people rushed to the house. Even though so many of our friends came over, as well as our pastor, it was still the longest and loneliest afternoon of my life. I am sure there were people who said some very kind words, but I just didn't hear them. I was in a fog—things were going on all around me, but I just wasn't comprehending what they were.

That night my mother's and my father's parents flew in from Texas. Dad's folks, Beverly and Ted Hillman, lived in Plano, a suburb of Dallas. My mom's parents, Jean and Bill Singleton, lived in the tiny town of Irene, about an hour south of Dallas. The seven or eight times I had visited Texas, I'd always loved staying with Grandfather and Grandmother Hillman. They had money, and there were all kinds of things to do where they lived and in nearby Dallas-Fort Worth. In my mind, they were cool.

I loved my mother's folks too, but Grandpa and Grandma Singleton were far from "cool." They lived on a farm in a small white-frame house. All that surrounded them were fields and more fields. Irene, the closest town, was four miles away and had about two hundred people. Except for the main road through town, the streets weren't even paved. I'd always told my friends that Irene should have been named "Nothingsville" because that's what was there—nothing. I could never figure out why Mom liked going back there so much.

The three days after my folks' death were little more than a blur for me. I remember the funeral, but I just don't remember talking to anyone. I also don't remember eating or sleeping either. I guess I was still too much in shock to fathom what was really happening. Only at the graveside, after the final prayer had been said and the minister handed me a rose off my mother's casket, did it really dawn on me that I'd never see my parents again. As tears flowed from my eyes, I fiddled with that red flower and wondered what would happen next. *At least, things can't get any worse.* How wrong I was.

CHAPTER 4

My grandparents from Plano left the day after the funeral. Grandfather had to get back to his law offices. As they were semi-retired and had rented most of their farmland out to neighbors, Grandpa and Grandma Singleton stayed in Chicago with me to sort out the legal stuff. It was the middle of May, and I had another two weeks before the spring term ended. I had to admit being back at school did help. I could escape there. The memories I had made at Franklin Delano Roosevelt Middle School were all mine. With my friends around me, I could put my grief on the backburner and pretend everything was as it always was. Still, each day, after the last bell, when I went home, the pain and loneliness were always there waiting for me. It hurt so bad to walk through my front door and not see or hear Mom and Dad. With each passing day, I found the void growing larger not smaller.

To escape the oppressing atmosphere at home, I often hit the tennis courts. I'd been to tennis camps since I was five. I was the best player in school and had twice placed second in my age division in the Chicago city championships. Along with hanging out at the Richfield Shopping Mall, skateboarding in White's Park, and scoring goals for the Swords in soccer, tennis was my life. I couldn't imagine what life would be like without it.

In the days after my parents' deaths, my tennis improved. I think this was because I was focusing on the game to try to block out the dark cloud filling the rest of my life. My backhand was as good as it had always been, but now my overhand was vicious and my ball placement better than ever. I also had a thirst to win that never seemed to be satisfied. I challenged anyone who would play with me no matter their age. Yet, even when I wiped out an opponent, I couldn't bring myself to smile. I was on top of my game, but not enjoying playing. Tennis just happened to be the best escape I could find—a way to channel my pain and anger. I used tennis to put off facing the real loss that was consuming me a little more each day.

When I was home, time was my enemy, as was everything else from the pictures on the walls to the clothes in my folks' closets. I quickly grew to hate the personal things that surrounded me when I was "trapped" in my own house.

As the days became weeks, I discovered just how much I had taken my parents for granted. I missed Dad's stupid stories. How I missed the hot breakfast Mom made me each day before school. And watching sports on television or playing video games wasn't as much fun now either. I didn't realize how much I had laughed with them or how much they had encouraged me to work toward my dreams. Anytime I had needed them, they had been there. They had let me live my life, but they were always around watching out for me too. That used to bug me, but now all I wished was for one of them to come marching into my room and say, "Have you done your homework?"

On June 1st, a hot, humid spring day, my dad's parents flew back from Texas and joined Grandpa and Grandma Singleton and me at the law offices of Jones, McFarland, and O'Leary. I didn't know as I walked into the company's suite on the forty-fifth floor of the Sears Tower, that this day would disrupt and change my life as much as my parents' deaths had.

Jennings McFarland, dressed in a fancy gray suit, white shirt, and blue tie, sat behind his desk and read through my parents' will. I was so caught up in that sinking feeling of loneliness that I paid little attention to the formalities of property division and the stuff about debts and net worth. But I was brought back to the present when Mr. McFarland said, "And now to discuss what will become of Thomas Dean Hillman."

As my eyes met his, the attorney nodded his head, and then further reviewed the document he held in front of him.

"Tommy, your parents left instructions in their will that if anything were to happen to them, you would go and live with your paternal or maternal grandparents."

Mr. McFarland paused to study my reaction, and then the realization hit me I'd have to leave the only home I had ever known. Chicago, my school, and my friends, not to mention all the familiar and wonderful places that been an integral part of my life, were going to be jerked away from me. I wouldn't be going to Wrigley Field and watching the Cubs a dozen times a year. I wouldn't be playing in the city tennis tourney. I wouldn't be listening to my favorite radio stations or walking downtown past the world famous Marshall Fields Department Store.

Yet, even as I mourned my latest round of losses, I came to grips with the fact Dallas wouldn't be that much different from Chicago. I consoled myself knowing while my parents would not be with me, my new life would be a lot like the one I had here. There were tennis courts and tournaments there, as well as a major league baseball team, malls, and lots of things to do. When I'd visited the city through the years, I'd even met some of the kids around where my grandparents lived. A sense of calm rushed over me as I realized I could adjust. After all, I'd always liked visiting Plano. And Grandfather and Grandmother's house was large and nice. I'd have a great room. They lived in one of the best neighborhoods in the city. As I put this news into perspective and grew more upbeat, Mr. McFarland continued.

"Quoting from the will: 'We, James and Kathleen Hillman, feel that having Tommy live with his grandparents on the farm outside of Irene would be the most special gift we could give him. In the country, he can experience a life few children get to know in this day and time. On the Singleton farm, Tommy will grow in new ways and directions, and we will know he will also be able to hold to the values that we treasure. Grandpa and Grandma's farm will be a place he can build the life and character that will help him make his dreams come true.'"

I felt as if I had been hit by a punch from the heavyweight champion of the world. I was stunned, too stunned to even talk. I knew, in death, my parents had surely made the biggest mistake of their lives. I was certain living on the farm wouldn't be the beginning of a wonderful new life—it would be the end of everything I cared about and loved. As I studied the faces in the room with me, I felt as if I'd died too. Irene, Texas, offered nothing to me, not even hope. Yet, I didn't say anything. Nor did I speak a word as we all rode back home in one car. What could I say? Everything had been decided without even consulting me.

CHAPTER 5

As soon as we returned to my house, I changed clothes and walked over to the courts. For the next hour, I slammed tennis balls into a backboard as hard as I could. Exhausted, I finally sat down on a bench to catch my breath and do some thinking. I'd decided running away was the only option I had when Ginny Patterson, a girl I often played tennis with, walked up to the court and sat down beside me.

"How are you doing?" she asked.

"Lousy," I shot back. "I'm moving to Texas to live with my grandparents. That's what the will said. I have no choice."

Her blonde hair shining in the afternoon sun, Ginny replied, "I thought you liked Dallas. That's what you have always told me."

"Oh, I do," I spit out the words bitterly, "but my parents decided I was going to stay with my other grandparents, the ones who live on the farm. It's the end of the world."

Ginny studied me for a moment, then, with a tone both sympathetic and optimistic, she added, "Tommy, your parents loved you. You know how cool I thought they were. They always knew what was best for you. Hey, whenever I was confused, they even knew what was best for me. If they decided you needed to live in the country, then I'm sure a lot of thought went into their decision. You just have to make the best of it."

"Like there is a best in this," I replied, hopelessness obvious in my tone and expression. "You won't be there, neither will anyone else I know. My grandparents are in their seventies, so are their friends. It's over. My life is really over. Don't you get it?"

Again and again, I hit my racket against the ground while Ginny's eyes locked on a match that was taking place on a nearby court, though I don't think she was really watching the game. I believe she was trying to find the words to make me feel better. After an awkward three minutes, she finally broke the silence.

"You can email me."

"Yeah, like Grandpa and Grandma are wired."

Ignoring my pessimistic response, she continued, "And I know you well enough to know you'll find something there that'll make you happy. After all, your mother was from this place. It can't be that bad."

Though I wanted to scream, instead I shook my head and laughed sarcastically, "You wouldn't say that if you'd been to Irene. It's like a vacuum, a place where people go and just fade away. And I guess that's what I'm going to do, just fade away."

I got up from the bench and began the walk home. I didn't look back, didn't acknowledge Ginny with even a word of farewell. I felt like a prisoner on his way to his a life sentence. I just knew in a few days when my grandparents and I got on the plane to Texas, it'd be the last time I would ever be in Chicago again. The final days of my real life were slipping away. Anger and bitterness replaced the sadness, and I just knew that I'd never be happy again.

CHAPTER 6

Irene, Texas was as different from Chicago as a T-Rex is from modern man. And in my mind, at least at that time, Irene was just as prehistoric as that ancient lizard. The tiny Texas community had a post office, a general store, a community church, and a school—not that I got to see them much. I spent most of my time five miles away down a dusty gravel road. From my initial view, I really believed my room overlooked the end of the world.

My grandparents' farm was probably pretty much the same as when my mother was a kid. The old frame two-story house was white with blue shutters, the barn hadn't been painted in years, and what little paint was left on the wood had faded dark red. The gate didn't work, the fence was falling down, and there was a beat up old tractor I was sure hadn't been used in years parked just beyond the barn. Their mailbox was mounted on an old wagon wheel. Grandpa thought it was cool—I was convinced it was the dumbest thing I had ever seen. As my grandparents were retired and renting out their cropland to another man, about all they raised now were chickens. Naturally, the first chore I was drew was gathering the eggs of the overgrown park pigeons. Though I didn't complain about scaring the cackling birds off nests and tossing out corn for food, I thought it would have been much easier to purchase a dozen eggs and use the hens for dinner. But what I thought didn't matter.

My spare hours—and I had plenty—were spent either watching the three channels that came in on the stone-age twenty-three inch console television setting in the living room, reading the daily Waco paper, or day dreaming about my old times in Chicago. When I got really bored, I kicked a soccer ball around the yard some or hit tennis balls against the barn wall. But by July, when the hot Texas sun began to send temperatures into the 100s, I pretty much camped out next to the window air conditioner in my room. After four or five days of temperatures hitting the century mark, I became convinced that Texas was not fit for human life. Little did I know that was just the beginning: August was when it *really* got hot!

Unlike in the city, where each day seemed to offer a new adventure and the chance to be with scores of friends, here time dragged by. Each protracted day was just like the one before—long, hot, and boring. Only Sunday broke the monotony. That was when we went to church. While church had been kind of fun in Chicago, scores of kids planning ski trips and other outings, the activities in Irene were a bit more limited to say the least. As a matter of fact, my grandparents' church only had about thirty members. When I arrived, I *was* the youth department. There were no other kids within ten years of my age! Most of the members were from the same generation as my grandparents. In my mind, God must have forgotten about this place and moved on too. I figured He'd wised up and was hanging in Chicago with my past life and friends.

As the summer crept by, I began to realize I was lost in a void, trapped in a world where I was the only kid. I grew so depressed I often wished I had been killed in the car wreck with my parents. As I drowned in pity, my grandparents tried to make me feel better, but they couldn't help. They didn't know how. Just when I thought my life could get no worse, the time came to start school.

CHAPTER 7

I carried not only a book bag but a huge chip on my shoulder that first day in the ancient brick building. Even before I walked through the doors, I was convinced the kids at this school were hicks. Even before I met them, I just knew I was going to hate them. I wasn't ready to even give them a chance. So, with an attitude like that, how could I have gotten off to a good start? Grandpa drove to me the building in the twenty-year-old Ford pickup that served as the family car. As he dropped me off, I set my jaw and walked toward the building's front door with anger etched deeply into my face, looking almost as if I were looking for a fight, and as it turned out, I all but found one.

The school in Irene was unlike anything I had ever seen. All grades, from kindergartners to seniors in high school, were taught in the same old brick building. And while the kids looked liked the ones in Chicago, meaning they came in all colors and sizes, I quickly found out they were a great deal different here in the sticks. For one thing, they didn't live in neighborhoods or apartments. The majority lived on farms. They didn't listen to the latest rap or rock music—they were tuned into country. Their clothes didn't really make it either. Nothing they wore came from Gap or Old Navy—the guys were sporting blue jeans and simple shirts. Worse yet, even the girls dressed that way.

On that initial day of class in late August, I felt as if every eye was on me—like I was being measured for a suit. Folks who'd been talking to their friends on the grounds and in the hallway suddenly stopped and stared. I'd never felt so uncomfortable. One kid, an upperclassman with sandy colored hair, a hundred freckles, a big nose, and crooked teeth kind of grinned at me for a second. I even thought he might be someone who wanted to be friends with the cool kid from Illinois, but I found out different when he laughed and then pointed toward me.

"Must be the new kid!"

He said it as if he were landing a jab in a boxing match. He wanted the comment to sting—to put me in my place. I guess I should've just blown him off and walked on, but his words, combined with a dozen kids closely studying me, got under my skin. I dropped my backpack and rushed over to him. I was determined to show him who was the boss. Yet, when I was standing directly in front of him, I discovered I was about six inches shorter and sixty pounds lighter than my antagonist. I had to save face, so I didn't back down, but I sure wish I'd thought before I acted. Pulling myself up as straight as I could, I snarled back, "Yeah, I'm the new kid. What's it to you? You want some of the new kid, do you?"

He just looked down at me for a moment, a somewhat shocked expression framing his green eyes, then a grin slowly covered his face. Finally, he shook his head and said, "Don't think I've ever had a city boy try to take me down before."

As I held my ground, he laughed and the others joined him. I had never been so humiliated or angry.

"Tell you what, Sonny," he finally added in a now disingenuously good-natured tone, "why don't you just come back in a few years when you grow up." He then pushed past me and casually strolled down the hallway, not even bothering to glance back in my direction.

For a few seconds, I stood in the middle of the school foyer, upset and confused, feeling like a pretty large fool. I was angry at the kid for singling me out but also angry at myself for reacting the way I did. I continued to stew for at least a minute more before a girl's voice brought me back to reality.

"You want your backpack?" she asked.

"Huh?" I replied as I turned around.

"Your backpack," the petite brunette replied. "You dropped it in the middle of the hall. Just thought you might want it."

I studied the girl for a moment. She was pretty in an uncomplicated sort of way. She had long hair, deep blue eyes, and a face that had seen some summer sun. The tan went nicely with her bright smile and white teeth. She was dressed in jeans, old tennis shoes, and a tee shirt. And while she couldn't have been much over five feet tall and probably didn't weigh a hundred pounds, her toned arms told me that she could probably take care of herself in a scrap.

"Why did you get in Johnny's face?" she asked as she handed me my blue bag.

"He mouthed at me," I replied.

"He was just pointing out that you'd arrived. I mean, we all knew you were coming. You *are* the new kid."

"What do you mean by that?" I shot back.

"I mean, you're the first new student we've had in a couple of years. It's kind of a big deal here in Irene when someone moves in."

"We had a new kid every day in the school I went to in Chicago. Sometimes five or six."

"Not here," she replied. "Most of us have gone to school with each other since kindergarten. Anyway, I know you're Tommy or Tom—the whole school knows that. Even the little kids. My name is Satara."

What kind of name was that? I mean, we had some strange handles in the Windy City, but nothing that strange. I shook my head as I eyed the girl who seemed to want to be my friend and shrugged. Finally I noted, "That name's a new one to me. I've never heard of Satara."

"My mom was a fan of the movie *Gone With The Wind*," she explained. "You ever seen it?"

"No," I replied. I had no idea what she was talking about.

"Well," Satara explained, "you should watch it, and then you'll understand where my name came from. Now, do want us to call you Tom, Tommy, or something else?"

"Tommy's fine."

"Ok, Tommy it is! I'll pass along the word, and by the end of the day, everyone will know that's the way you want it. And lighten up some—we all just want you to fit in. As few folks as we have around here, we can't afford to waste any of them."

Satara's voice, with its Texas twang, blew me away. I loved the way her words tumbled from her lips. As she walked me down the hall to my locker, telling me about some of the teachers and how bad the lunchroom food was, I wondered if I'd like to listen to her as much if she hadn't been such a babe. Even by Chicago standards, she was dynamite.

Besides Satara, who was one of the eleven kids in the freshman class with me, I didn't really get to know many folks my first few weeks at school. They were nice enough, but we didn't have much in common and, whenever I got the chance, I loved to point that out. They talked about cows and pigs, the dances at the fire hall, the bingo games at the Catholic Church, and the football and volleyball games. I didn't know much about any of those things, and I cared even less. So at lunch, I just sat there and listened to everyone else talk. One day, a sophomore boy, Greg James, finally got around to asking me what kind of sports I played back the city. It was the first time someone had really wanted to know anything about my old life. With the door opened, I eagerly charged through it.

"Tennis and soccer, mainly," I quickly answered.

"Soccer?" they all asked at once.

"Yeah," I bragged. "I was the captain of my team. We finished second in the city playoffs."

"*Soccer?* Isn't that a game for little kids?" Greg cut in with a grin.

"No," I quickly shot back, "we even have a team in high school. All my friends play on it."

"Still sounds like a sissy game to me," he laughed. "Now football, *that's* a man's game. You have to be tough to play that. Which I guess is why a city boy like you didn't come out for the team."

Before I could snap off one of my sarcastic replies, Satara cut in, "Listen, things were different up North. They have more choices than we do. Besides, we might not play soccer, but we used to have a tennis team."

"Used to?" I asked.

"Yeah," Greg laughed, "but when they couldn't get anybody to come out for the squad, they took down the nets and turned it into the school bus parking lot."

As everyone laughed, I glanced out the lunchroom window toward the place where I had seen the buses parked. As I looked at the concrete, I noted a few faded lines. The playing surface was uneven and chipped, and oil from leaks in the busses had dripped all over it. I wondered how many years since anyone had played there.

"So what about it, Tommy?" another boy named Luke cut in, "Why don't you come out for football?"

I shook my head, still staring out toward the busses.

"At least come to the game this week," Mindy Jo, one of Satara's friends pleaded. "I mean, we've had three already, and you haven't been to any of them."

"No," I replied. "I don't think so."

"Why not?" Luke shot back. "Everyone is there. It's a big deal here in town. You're the only student in the whole high school that doesn't go. Hey, each of us participates too. I mean, those who aren't on the field cheer, film, keep stats, work in the concession stand, or sell programs. Why don't you start pulling your weight?"

"There's no rule that says I have to," I answered. "I have to go to school here in this forgotten hole—I think that's enough."

CHAPTER 8

After I had said those words, everyone grew real silent, but their expressions told me all I needed to know. My hastily formed words had painted me into a corner. For the rest of the meal, no one said much at all, yet I knew they were digesting what I'd spit out. I knew it wasn't going down well either. Later in the day, after the last bell when Satara and I were putting our books in our lockers, she brought up the subject of tennis again.

"Why don't you tell Coach Boyd you want to go out for tennis this year? I'm sure he could find the nets and get them to park the buses somewhere else. I always wanted to learn how to play, maybe I could go out too."

"I don't know," I answered. "I mean, those old courts look pretty far gone. I wouldn't have even thought about playing on something in that kind of condition when I was in Chicago." Those words proved the ones that would break even the bond that had developed between the cute brunette and myself.

Slamming her locker, showing frustration for the first time since I'd met her, Satara looked me straight in the eyes and growled, "Tell you what, Tommy Hillman, over the past month you've constantly told me how much better things were in Chicago. And when you've not talked about Chicago, you've complained about how you should have gotten to live in Dallas rather than here. The other kids have been pretty nice to you, but they're getting tired of the way you run everything down. I'll admit we don't have much here in Irene. About all we really have is each other and our pride. In fact, the only way we have enough kids for a six-man football team is that about all the boys go out. And they work hard, not because we have the best field or new uniforms, but because those boys want to make all of us who are watching proud. The same goes for volleyball, basketball, baseball, and even the one-act play. All of us have to pull our weight to make things happen here. If we don't, then nobody gets to do much. You could make an impact if you'd just try to work with us rather than staying by yourself. You could probably even bring back the tennis program. But if we aren't good enough for you, and if Irene is not good enough for you, then that's fine."

She paused, shook her head and took a breath before she sadly noted, "It looks to me like you decided your life ended when you left the city. I'm sorry your folks died. I feel you, I really do. But I want you to chew on this. Our town cemetery is on your way home. Why don't you stop there and bury yourself, because you've clearly decided you're too good to live here with us. Now, I have to go volleyball practice, and I guess your grandparents are out there waiting to take you back home."

I grabbed Satara by the arm, stepping in front of her to block her exit. Looking into her deep blue eyes, I proved how stupid I was again. Once more I didn't think before opening my mouth. The words that flew out simply confirmed what she and the rest of the school already believed.

"Listen, I had everything a kid could want in Chicago. It was a great place, things were always happening. I didn't ask to come to Hicksville and go to school in a place that's so old the flagpole probably used to fly a flag with about thirty stars. I just got stuck here. And as far as pride in old Irene, I don't see anything anyone could ever have much pride in. This place is the end of the world. And I've seen the real world, the one you can't even imagine, so I know that for a fact. I'm sorry you think so much of this place because it shows just how shallow and deprived you are. I have to go to school here, and I'll do that until I can find a way out, but I don't have to be a part of anything that goes on here. Think how pathetic it is you're going to a school that plays six-man football. That's not real football. When was the last time anyone who played a Mickey Mouse game like that ended up doing anything more than bailing hay for a living? So give me a break and get off my back. I don't need your speeches, your little world, or your little thoughts."

Though she must have been angry, Satara didn't say a word. She simply shook her head and slipped by me on her way to practice. I guess I shouldn't have been surprised when the next morning, she didn't speak to me in the hallway, didn't look at me during classes, and sat on the other side of the cafeteria during lunch. Things didn't change the next day or the next week, either. And by Christmas, I was pretty much shunned by everyone. They'd grown tired of trying to make me one of the group. I was now just the weird city kid. And for the moment, that was just the way I wanted it.

CHAPTER 9

Not long after holidays, Coach Boyd came up to ask me if I wanted him to clean up the tennis courts and start a tennis team. I told him I had no interest at all. And that was true. I really had no desire in anything by then. I was just marking time. My grades had fallen to the point where I was barely passing, I'd pretty much given up writing to my old friends in Chicago, and I didn't even talk much to my grandparents. About all I looked forward to and greeted with any enthusiasm was going to see my grandparents in Dallas. Those weekends reminded me a little bit about how great my life had been before my parents died. Those days also showed me how bad my life had become now. One Sunday afternoon in April, when I was riding around in the big city with Grandpa Hillman, I actually thought I was about to receive a second chance at a new life.

"You haven't been happy in Irene, have you?" he suddenly noted.

"No," I quickly replied, "I hate it. You just can't imagine what it's like to live in a place with nothing going for it."

"Not much of a country boy are you?" he observed.

"Not at all," I agreed. "I don't like the town or the people."

Grandpa was a big man, well over six feet tall and weighing in at about two hundred and fifty. His eyes were dark brown, his skin chalky, and his hair thinning. He always wore a suit and he was also always serious. Yet, at this moment, he was even more serious than normal.

"Your grades are horrible," he said dryly. "And I hear you don't have any friends."

I suddenly realized I had an opening. If I played my cards right, I might just get a chance to move in with he and Grandma Hillman. Trying to sound both sincere and mournful, I began, "If I lived with you all, I know things would be so different. You can't imagine what it's like there.

There is only one plug in my whole room. Mom's parents don't even own a computer or a cell phone. It's like I'm living in the Dark Ages."

"Your grandparents tell me you don't have any friends either," he added. "They say you are usually sullen, and you never smile or laugh."

"I would say they're pretty close to right," I admitted. His next words thrilled me to my core.

"They think it might be better if you came to live with us before the next school year. What do you think?"

"Yeah," I all but shouted, a smile leaping onto my face for the first time in months. "I really feel I need to be up here. If I was with you and Grandma in Plano, I know I could make lots of friends, play soccer and tennis, and bring my grades up."

"So you think," Grandfather Hillman added, "that your folks made a mistake placing you with the Singletons?"

I didn't answer right away. In fact, his words caught me off guard. I hadn't really considered my parents in all this. Now I realized if I left the farm and came to Dallas, I'd actually be putting the blame on them for making a terrible decision. It'd be like saying they were the ones who'd made me so unhappy. I wondered what they would think of my doing that? Would they be hurt because I didn't love the farm and Irene like Mom had? I chewed on that for a second before the picture of that horrible school leaped back into my head. They'd died on me, so what did it matter? I didn't desert them—they deserted me. So, what they might have thought didn't matter as much as my own happiness. It was time for a move. Still, even, as I formed my answer, I couldn't shake the thought of disappointing them.

"Yeah," I almost whispered, like I was afraid my folks would hear me. "This time, I guess they were wrong."

We drove along in silence by all the places I wanted have in my life— soccer fields, shopping malls, and fast food joints—until we finally pulled up into Grandfather Hillman's driveway. Before he got out, he looked over at me and made a promise. "You go back to Irene this evening. You stick it out at school for the rest of the term. Then in June, you can come up here and live with us."

I was so happy I could have shouted. This was the best news I'd received in the past year. Finally, I would be given the chance to live my dreams and escape the nightmare that was Irene, Texas. Finally, the city boy would come home!

CHAPTER 10

As the Texas winter winds sliced down the gravel road of my new home, and as the endless days of school dragged by, I counted down the days until I could get out of the country and back to the city. Spring came, the bluebonnets bloomed and crops were planted. The weather grew warmer, and I became happier. Then, just two weeks before school was to be let out, I was hit with another terrible blow. Grandpa Singleton picked me up after another long and boring day at school, and I could tell by the look on his weathered, sun-kissed face something was wrong. I had just closed the pickup's door when he began to speak.

"Your Grandfather Hillman had a heart attack today," he solemnly explained as he steered the truck down the dusty road to the farm.

I didn't speak for a few moments, too caught up in shock to fully understand the impact of the news. I finally managed to mutter, "Is he going to be all right?"

"They think so," came Grandpa's reply. "It'll take some time though and an operation too."

For the moment, I was just relieved he was alive. That was enough for the time being. A week later, after he made it through his open-heart surgery, that relief turned to anguish. He'd be fine, but it was going to take a while for him to get back on his feet, and Grandmother Hillman didn't think it'd be good for him to have a teenager in the house as he recovered. In other words, I was going to have to stay in Irene on the farm. My hopes, my dreams, and my plans once again turned into dust. All I could do was climb the steps up to my room at the farm, look out over the barren Texas landscape, and cry. For the second time in a year, I felt as if any chance I had for happiness was gone forever. Maybe Satara had been right. Maybe I should have just stopped at the Irene Cemetery and pulled the sod over my head. Yet, the same attitude that had made life so miserable for me during my freshman year in Irene would be responsible for giving me a second chance at the beginning of my sophomore year.

CHAPTER II

I'd been so bored during my second summer on the farm I almost looked forward to school starting. Of course, the operative word was *almost*. In truth, while I didn't want to deal with the kids, the teachers, the classes, or the homework, I did need a change of pace from the boring routine of my daily life.

The first few days of school were pretty much like the last few months had been the year before. I was all but shunned. Not that the kids avoided me—they just didn't make any effort to include me in any of their conversations. In class, in the hallway, and at lunch, they would nod their heads or say "Hey," but except for a senior named Josh, they just didn't say anything else.

Josh thought he was tough and loved to prove it. He was a big guy, maybe six-foot-three, his fleshy face framed by a mop of curly dark black hair. I figured he must be pretty strong, but his muscles were well-hidden by at least forty pounds of fat. Josh had failed a few courses over the years, so even though he and I were two years apart in age, we shared a lab table in chemistry class. I never did find out if this was the second or third time he'd been forced to take the course.

I'd never met anyone who loved to needle me as much as Josh did. For the first days, I just ignored him and pretended to be deaf. But after a while, his vocal jabs began to really get to me. Little did I know, the negativity coming out of Josh's mouth would finally get me started on a new positive path, but that's exactly what happened just one week into the new school year.

"Hillman," Josh begin that Monday at lunch, "you're the biggest wimp that has ever come into this school."

Like I had during the previous week, I tried to ignore him. Yet, as he was now speaking loudly enough for everyone to hear, I couldn't ignore the fact the words really ate at me. And he wouldn't shut up. Every time he tossed out another sentence, I felt like he was slapping me across my face.

"There isn't a girl in this school who couldn't beat you at anything you tried to do," he nearly shouted. Then he laughed and added, "Oh, that's right, you don't try anything do you?"

I continued to look down, studying the sandwich and chips on my plate, trying my best to control my temper. Yet, his next barb ended any reserve I had left.

"I know why you're an orphan too." Though I pretended not to, I listened closely, wondering where he was taking this line of talk. His next taunt put me over the edge.

"Yeah, your folks died because they simply couldn't live with the yellow low life they'd created."

I took no more than two seconds to leap up from my seat, clear the lunch table between us knocking trays and food everywhere, and land a solid right cross to Josh's jaw. He fell like a load of bricks back into the wall behind him. The stunned look on his face assured me that I'd surprised him. Realizing that he could probably beat the stuffing out of me if I gave him time to regroup, I again closed the distance between us and landed four more blows. The first three found his fleshy belly while the last one caught him square in the left eye. As two other students pulled me back, Josh teetered for a moment on his heels, then deflated like an old balloon. Less than a breath later, he was prone on the floor gasping for air, his ugly face twisted like a pretzel.

"What's going on here!" Mr. Miller, the school superintendent, demanded as he charged over to us. Looking down at Josh, who was still moaning on the ground, then over at me, my fists clenched and my jaw set and tight, I'm sure he quickly figured it all out. He waited a few more seconds, then shook his head, leaned over, and helped Josh to his feet.

"You going to be all right, boy?" the administrator asked the bully.

"Yeah," Josh answered, "he got in a lucky punch."

The superintendent quickly examined the swelling around Josh's jaw and eye and noted, "Must have been more than one." He then turned to me and said, "You did this?"

"Yes, sir," I smugly replied.

"He had it coming," Satara cut in. Some of the other students quickly agreed. Satara then told Mr. Miller what Josh had said. That was all it took.

Josh had not only taken his lumps from me, but he was also going to have to take them from Mr. Miller.

"Josh, I want to see you in my office," the superintendent announced. The small middle-aged man with the wire-framed glasses then turned to me. "Meanwhile, Tommy, we don't solve disputes in this school with violence. I understand why you responded the way you did, but you still have to be punished. I'll let Coach Boyd decide what you need to do to learn your lesson. You'll check in with him during PE."

"You just watch your back boy," Josh cut in as he glared at me through his black eye. "If you had the guts to come out for football, I'd pay you back on the field. But wimps like you only hit when folks aren't looking. Football's not your kind of game. You're too scared!"

Even though I'd won the fight, Josh's words still stung. Everyone knew that on the gridiron, he'd probably inflict a lot more damage to me than I just had to him. I also realized the next time he caught me off school grounds, he'd try to even the score as well. And in a fair fight, he could do it too. I was really trapped.

CHAPTER 12

"You won the first battle," Satara noted as I picked up my books from my locker at the end of the day, "but you didn't win the war. I've seen Josh wrestle a steer at the rodeo. He'll get even—and then some. I don't think you need to be by yourself for a while. You might even want to buy a big dog."

Her words chilled me to the bone. Now, I desperately wished I had ignored what he said—just gone on eating my lunch and pretending to be deaf. Yet, because in one way he had been right, I had to fight. I knew Mom and Dad wouldn't have been proud of how I'd been acting. They would have been disappointed in my attitude, my behavior, my grades, and my lack of motivation. The fact even someone as slow-witted as Josh knew that really brought things into focus for me too. I needed to change, but I didn't really know how to begin. And for the moment I didn't have time to worry about that. I had to meet with Coach Boyd and hear what my punishment was going to be.

The coach's office was nothing more than a tiny cedar block cubicle just outside the boy's locker room and always smelled like well-used towels. I figured the last time it'd really been cleaned was when my mom had been in school and probably hadn't been painted since my grandfather was a student. As I walked in, Coach Boyd was studying a notebook filled with Xs and Os. At the time, that language meant nothing to me—later I'd discover this was the Bible of the gridiron—the playbook.

"Mr. Miller told me to come see you," I mumbled as I ambled through the coach's open door.

Boyd was about fifty, a rock solid one-eighty, and about five-feet-nine. His hair was a mixture of red and gray, his eyes green, and his lips thin. When he spoke, he always waved his hands.

"Hillman," he grinned as he looked up. "You put some hurt on Jenkins today. I haven't seen a shiner like that in years."

"Yes, sir," I responded, not knowing if I needed to smile or act ashamed. Confused, I did neither.

"I mean, he wasn't much to look at before," the coach continued, "but now, well, when I was a kid I had a hog … I guess you probably don't want to hear that story."

I just shrugged and waited, standing in front of the desk, looking for all the world like a condemned man hoping for a reprieve.

"Here is the deal, Hillman," he explained as he got up from his desk. "I need someone to help me with the equipment during the season. Your job will be to pick up the locker room after practice, help me wash the uniforms, sweats, and shirts, and give the players water during practice and games."

I couldn't believe what I was hearing. I figured I'd have to write a paper or maybe run some laps during PE. These duties meant I'd be at school even longer than the players. I'd also all but be Josh's slave. I couldn't think of anything any worse.

"Isn't there something else, coach?" I pleaded.

"There is one thing," came the stoic reply.

"What?" I blurted.

"Prove Jenkins and the rest of this school wrong. Go out for football." He paused, waved a hand at me, and added, "Use the moves you learned in soccer in Chicago on the field for the Wampus Cats. I saw Jenkins—I know you can move and hit. I bet you're already the best kicker on the team too."

"I don't know, Coach," I stammered. "I mean, I've never even seen a six-man football game. I'd be so far behind the rest of the kids."

"Yeah," he admitted, "you've missed two weeks of practice and years of fundamentals, but John and Aaron are playing this year for the first time too. And besides, Josh is going to want to get you back for what you did to him. At least on the football field, you'd have pads on when he cornered you. You go on home now and think about it, and you can give me your answer tomorrow."

At supper, I told my grandparents I'd decided to go out for football. I didn't tell the reason for my decision or about the fight. I figured they would find out both of those stories in time. By then, maybe I could come up with some explanation that would help me plead my case. I also left out that the only reason I was really going out was to avoid being a water boy and to get to wear pads when Josh took me to the cleaners.

That night I barely slept. I was a little bit scared, *a lot* intimidated, and very much confused. I had no idea what to expect.

CHAPTER 13

I avoided Josh all day, and that afternoon after seventh period, I was back in Coach Boyd's office. He seemed happy I'd decided to play. After digging out pads and a practice uniform, he led me out onto the football field.

"Well, look who's here," Josh bellowed out when he saw me, "it's the city wimp. Well, soccer boy, I have you now!"

An hour later, after going through strange drills I found a mystery, I was lining up for my first play. Coach had me playing corner for the defense. I had no idea what I was supposed to do. Suddenly, even as I was trying to figure out how to stand, the ball was snapped, the quarterback pitched it to the tailback, and all six men on offense headed in my direction. I held my ground for a moment, trying to find the ball carrier. Then a huge body blocked my view. I looked up just in time to see a grinning Josh Jenkins bearing down on me as fast as his thick legs would carry him. This time, I was the one who didn't respond quickly enough. I don't even remember being hit, I just recall lying flat on my back, gasping for air as my eyes tried to focus on the cloudless blue sky above my head. In the background, I heard a bunch of voices screaming, "Great block, Josh!" I also heard the giant laughing.

Though it seemed like every bone in my body was crying out for mercy, I ignored the pain, bounced to my feet, and turned to face the man who had just knocked me down. Grinning, I looked right at Josh's facemask and helmet and shouted, "You can sure hit hard!"

The big guy studied me for a second, then laughed. "I'll do it again, too." I had no doubt he would. Still, I also felt our private war was over. I'd taken his best shot and gotten up. In his mind, that made us even.

From that time on, I didn't have any problem with Josh. He'd expected to roll me over and to watch me quit. When I'd bounced back up and congratulated him, he somehow decided I was all right. Within a few days, the rest of the kids seemed to believe the same thing too. I even thought they started to take it easy on me. Of course, that may have been because by then they'd discovered I was the best kicker they had. In truth, I think that is the real reason the coach wanted me to come out.

Other than using five fewer players, I discovered during my initial week of practice six-man football was not much different than the regular game. I later found out rules varied from state to state, but the sport was still pretty basic football: kick, catch, block, tackle, and score. In Texas, the quarterback couldn't advance the ball beyond the line of scrimmage—he had to hand off or pass. Everyone, including the center, was eligible to catch a pass. The field was only eighty yards long. A team had to go fifteen yards for a first down, and a kicked extra point was worth two points. In my mind, the very best rule was a field goal counted for four points. Yet, I quickly learned with three people directly involved in each kick—the kicker, the holder, and the snapper—and only three other guys left to block the six defenders, getting a kick off the tee and through the uprights was not easy. I was going to have to work on doing it a lot more quickly than I would have in the eleven-man game or even on a soccer field.

On the Friday of the game with Birome, I got my uniform. My number was 6. Like the rest of the team, I wore the jersey to my classes that day and walked out in front of the school at the pep rally. As I listened to the whole student body cheer, I felt for the first time like I was really a part of Irene. But that sense of pride confused me at the moment. I guess I didn't want to admit this tiny place could give me something I had not ever felt or experienced in Chicago. And yet, that's exactly what had happened.

CHAPTER 14

That night, as I ran onto the field for the first time, I was so excited I could barely speak. My knees were weak in the pre-game drills, and I thought I was going to collapse from nerves during "The National Anthem." Still, I couldn't wait to get on the field. But it wouldn't happen that night. We didn't score, and I never got the chance to kick an extra point. The Birome Bears beat us 42 to nothing. Losing hurt.

After I took my shower and changed into my street clothes, I walked back out onto the field. The scoreboard and the lights had been turned off, and I thought I was alone. As I looked over the west goal post at the starry Texas night, a voice seemed to come out of nowhere and land in my head.

"I'm proud of you, Tommy."

I turned, and in the dim light I saw Satara coming toward me. She was still wearing her green and white cheerleader uniform.

"Hi," I smiled.

"Hi, yourself," she answered.

"We got beat," I observed. "It doesn't feel very good. I hate losing!"

"You get used to it," Satara announced very matter-of-factly, "that's what Irene does. We lose. For years, other teams have called us the Wampus Kittens rather than the Wampus Cats. Our football has been bad for so long it's no longer a joke, but rather, a tradition."

"Oh," I sighed. "Maybe that'll change."

"Are you going to change it?" she asked.

"Do you think I can?"

Satara didn't answer. Instead, she reached out, took my left hand in her right, and began to walk me off the field. When we got to the stands, she finally turned and faced me, but she didn't let go of my hand.

"I think one person can make a difference," she explained, measuring her words as carefully as a carpenter measures a board before cutting.

"That's what my mom has always told me. She speaks from experience too. She was in a car wreck when she was in high school. She almost died. She was in the hospital for weeks. The doctors even told her that she'd never walk again. You see this medal I wear on my sweater?"

I looked down and noted the round piece of brass pinned to the big white and green "I." When Satara was convinced I had seen it, she continued.

"Well, a friend of hers told her she would not only walk again, but she'd run too. And over time, that friend convinced Mom. Thanks to her friend, my mom worked hard. Within a few months, she had tossed her crutches away. A year later, Mom even started running. The doctors considered that a miracle, but for Mom it wasn't enough. Her friend agreed and convinced her to go out for cross-country. She won the district that year and went to state the next."

"Wow!" I replied.

"Tommy, the person who convinced Mom that she could walk, then run, and then win, was your mother. She was the friend who pushed her, prodded her, and ran beside her."

I didn't know what to say. I was totally and completely caught off guard. My mom had made the difference in Satara's mom's life? She was the one who inspired her?

"Satara, it's time to go," a voice called out from the parking lot.

"That's my mom." Before running off, Satara turned to me and said, "Tommy, you can make a difference here. I think your mom must have known that when she and your dad put the Singletons in charge of you. See you at school on Monday."

As Satara walked off into the darkness toward her mother's car, I suddenly felt very different. For a moment, I could have sworn my mother was somewhere looking at me and smiling.

CHAPTER 15

Satara's words haunted me the rest of the weekend. They forced me to open up long-closed doors and deal with emotions I thought I'd buried. I even spent most of Sunday afternoon talking to my grandmother about my mother. I'd never really thought much about Mom as anything but a grown-up. When I started to learn that she'd been an athlete, a top student, a cheerleader, and the president of her class, I began to look at her in a different light. Yet, what impressed me more than any of those things was what Satara had told me. I vowed to get to know Satara's mother and have her share what she remembered about Mom.

For the next four weeks, my life was better than it had been since the long lost days in Chicago. I was really happy. I began to study hard, really got to know my fellow students, was friendlier and more outgoing than I had been in years, and worked hard in football practice trying to learn as much as I could fast as possible. I also got close to Satara again. And every week proved what she had told me after our game with Birome—no matter how hard we tried, we simply couldn't win a football game. To fully illustrate that point, in the next four games, I only got to kick two extra points. In two of the contests, the games ended early on what was called the "mercy rule." That meant if the other team got ahead by more than forty-five points by the end of the first half, the game was called "over." At Irene, just getting to play in the second half was a reason to celebrate.

The third week in October was Homecoming Week. The festivities were great. Each day we dressed in a different style of a past era, there were spirit posters pasted all over the school hallways, and in spite of our record, everyone was upbeat. I even worked up my nerve and actually asked Satara to go to the Homecoming Dance after the game with me. She accepted too. On Friday after the pep rally and school, Grandma took me to the nearest big town, Hillsboro, where I bought Satara the prettiest mum I could find. I was determined to make this night one of her best memories. But while I could control the flower and the way I danced, I suspected I would have little control over the outcome of the game. After all, the only thing I did was kick extra points, which happened rarely, and then, I'd just watch from the sidelines.

A crowd of several hundred rural folks filled the stands that evening as we took on the Brandon Buffaloes. Even though most of those from Irene wore green spirit ribbons and cheered us when we ran onto the field, I knew none of them expected us to win. After all, the last time Irene won a Homecoming game had been eleven years before. The standard joke was "at least the 'mercy rule' lets us start the dance early." In eight of the last ten games, that had proven true.

We opened with the ball. On the first play, Jeremy Hanna busted through the right side of the line for a five-yard gain. As the home fans cheered the unexpected positive yards, our guys jumped up and marched back to the huddle. But Jeremy didn't move. He remained on the ground. Coach Boyd and the school nurse Julie Hammock rushed out on the field. For the next couple of minutes, everyone waited for news. Finally, coach signaled two of us to come out and help Jeremy to the sidelines. They thought he might have torn his ACL. If that were the case, our number one running back would be out for the year.

Eric Birdwell moved over from end to running back, and we played on. It was an inspired effort. We even managed three first downs before the end of the initial quarter. Unfortunately, Brandon, led by their all-state running back, Andrew James, scored three touchdowns and ran in two extra points, so we were down 20-0.

We opened the second quarter with the ball on our own fifteen-yard line. On first down, Eric gained two yards. On the next play, he was hit almost as soon as Jimmy Chambers, the quarterback, handed him the ball. I knew he was hurt by the way he landed on the ground. The Buffalo defensive end had all but bent him in two. I was shocked Eric hadn't fumbled. When our ball carrier stayed down, the officials waved to the sidelines for the coach to come out. About a minute later, Eric came out of the game too. His right arm was broken just above the elbow.

As Nurse Haddock led Eric away, Coach Boyd called time out. He circled the ten of us who were left around him.

"Ok, let's regroup," he began. "We've been playing hard, but we've just gotten a couple of bad breaks." I remember thinking at the time that 'break' was probably a poor choice of words. I winced as he said it.

"What we're going to do now is move Tommy into the game at running back."

My jaw dropped.

CHAPTER 16

As stunned as the team was by coach's statement, I was even more taken aback. The only time I'd exhibited any ability to run on a football field was during wind sprints. True, I always won those, but I'd never even carried the ball once in practice. I was ignorant to a fault. Surely this had to be a joke. Or worse yet, maybe the coach figured if someone else was going to get hurt, I was the player who was most expendable.

"Tommy," Coach Boyd yelled to snap me out of my shocked daze and get my attention. "We're going to keep it simple. I know you don't know the plays. Just run through whatever holes you find. In soccer, you had to change directions in a hurry and react to the ball. Do the same thing here—just react to the guy who's trying to tackle you. You have a lot of speed. Hold onto the ball and run for your life."

I was scared to death. I was in such a state of shock I didn't even realize I'd run onto the field and a play had been called. As we broke the huddle, Jimmy pointed to the spot where I was supposed to stand. Two "huts" later, he was turning and flipping the ball my way.

After securing the pigskin in my hands, I looked up and spied not one, but two red-suited Buffs headed through the hole I was supposed to use. I wasn't stupid—I didn't want to get creamed. So I took one step to my right, then, just before the first one hit me, I did a 360° spin. Both defenders flew past me as I reversed direction and headed for the far side of the field. Passing the line of scrimmage, I spotted a defensive back on a pursuit angle to my left. Just as he got to me, I juked him with my shoulders, literally stopped in my tracks, and felt him glance off my hip pads. Hitting stride again, I raced past the thirty and forty, faked another man out at the Brandon thirty and suddenly realized I had clear sailing all the way to the end zone. Nine seconds and sixty-five yards after taking my first snap, I scored a touchdown. After kicking the extra point, the score was 20-8.

Our scoring seemed to inspire the six guys who anchored our defense. They stopped the Brandon offense on three plays. Coach Boyd sent me in to field the punt. I grabbed the ball at a full gallop on our own thirty. The blocking was incredible. I was in the end zone before I realized. An extra point kick later, the score was now 20-16. For the remainder of the half, we had a scoring duel. Greg Ledsome scored a touchdown on a nineteen-yard pass from Jimmy. I got another TD on a seventeen-yard run. Brandon and their star running back, James, got their licks in too, though. By the time the buzzer sounded, and we took a fifteen-minute halftime break, the scoreboard read Brandon 35, Irene 32.

The second half was more of the same—like a tennis match, back and forth, back and forth. I had once heard my grandfather call six-man football, "basketball on grass." I now realized he was right. When two teams are evenly matched and the offenses are hot, points seem to just flood the scoreboard. This kind of output leaves both the players and the fans breathless.

Surprising no one, Brandon scored four more touchdowns and hit each of their extra-point kicks. Surprising *everyone*, we matched them blow for blow. Greg caught one sixteen-yard scoring pass, and I somehow found holes and scored from the eighteen, twenty-two, and thirty-eight. With under a minute to go, we were down 72 to 69 and Brandon had the ball.

On a first and fifteen from their own thirty-six-yard line, the Buffalo quarterback handed to his two hundred and twenty-pound lumbering fullback. We only had one timeout left, so they didn't even have to make a first down. All Brandon was trying to do was run the clock out. As their big #34 hit the hole, our own mammoth dude came out of his nose tackle spot. Josh Jenkins met the back head on. As their helmets and pads hit, it sounded like a cannon blast. For a split-second they both held their ground, then the running back began to stumble. As he did, Josh ripped the pigskin out of his arms.

From the sidelines, it appeared that everything had suddenly slowed down. The ball almost floated above the huge mounds of sweaty flesh and hovered about six feet off the ground. As the tackler and the ball carrier fell, ten other boys scrambled across the grass toward the elusive, oblong, leather-covered ball. A Buffalo linemen got to it first, but the ball slipped through his hands. One of our guys knocked it out of the air, then the pigskin bounced along among a half-dozen other players, coming closer and closer to our sideline. Finally, just a few yards before it went out of bounds, Hector Rivas, one of our senior linebackers, leapt over a pile of bodies and literally engulfed the ball, rolling over on his back and lifting it in the air before he slid across the out-of-bounds lines. The crowd erupted, my mild-mannered grandmother's voice louder and stronger than any of the others. Now we had a chance!

Coach Boyd called us over and drew out a simple hook and ladder play. Jimmy would take the snap, drop three steps and throw the ball to Greg. He would catch it about five yards past the line of scrimmage, which was our own thirty-nine, and as the Buffalo tacklers charged toward him, he would flip the ball back to me. My job was to run up the sideline for another touchdown. As there were only twenty-seven seconds left on the clock, and we had just one time-out remaining, we couldn't afford any mistakes.

As diagrammed, Jimmy took the snap, faked it to me, and then made a perfect pass to Greg. I was racing toward him as he caught the ball. He tapped it back to me as if the pigskin was a volleyball and he was a setter. Though we had executed the play to perfection, not everyone had been fooled. The Brandon deep safety had seen it coming and was racing toward me with fire in his eyes. As soon as I caught the ball, he hit me. I never had a chance. I was dropped in my tracks.

Jimmy hurried us back to the line of scrimmage and gunned a pass into the ground to stop the clock. As we looked at third down, there were only ten seconds remaining and we still had to move thirty-seven yards for a touchdown. Coach Boyd signaled in a pass play. Jimmy hit Chris Thompson over the middle for ten yards, but he couldn't get out of bounds. I hurried up to an official and called time out. We were down to our last four seconds.

On the sideline, Coach Boyd drew up a halfback option pass. I was to flank out to the far left, Chris was to take my spot in the backfield. I needed to run as fast as I could and not even look for the ball until I was in the end zone. But before we could break the huddle and run back out onto the field, Josh piped up with another suggestion.

"Why don't we let Tommy kick a field goal?"

Coach looked at the big guy as if he had lost his mind.

"For starters, with the distance added for placement, the kick would be a forty-three-yard try," he explained. "Secondly, in the fifty-year history of six-man football at Irene, no one has ever kicked a field goal of any length. Every one that has ever been tried has been blocked. We wouldn't have a chance."

I couldn't believe my next words. "Coach, the city soccer player can do it. I can kick the ball that far and make it. And the line will block out their guys. I know that Josh can get the snap back in a hurry. We've been working on that for the past four weeks."

"You sure?" Coach Boyd asked as he looked at me sternly.

"If these guys will block for me," I assured him, "I can do it."

Coach looked out at the field for a second, then at the goal post. Shaking his head, he grinned. "They probably will think it's a fake and not rush anyway. Give it your best shot, kid."

Coach Boyd was right. As we lined up in field goal formation, Brandon remained in their normal defensive look. Our fans didn't believe we were going to kick any more than the Buffaloes did. Even as Josh snapped the ball to Jimmy and he placed it on the tee, everyone just kind of stood still. Sensing I had plenty of time, I approached the ball slowly, keeping my head low. I planted my left foot just ahead of the ball and swung through with my right. Like everyone else, I held my breath as the ball exploded off the tee. Three or four seconds later, it cleared the uprights, landing five yards beyond the end line. Perfect. The official signaled good, the gun went off, the game was over, and we had won 73-72. Yet, even as the points were tallied on the scoreboard, few cheered and hardly anyone moved. It was as if no one, including myself, believed what had just happened. *Thank goodness for four-point field goals. I couldn't have survived an overtime.*

Looking over at the sideline, I noted a cheerleader in a strange outfit jumping up and down. She was pretty and looked very familiar. "Way to go, Thomas!" she screamed. I wanted to take another look at her, but before I could, Josh raced up to me and hit me, knocking me to the ground. Soon he was joined by the other players, Coach Boyd, the cheerleaders, and seemingly the whole crowd. We'd won a Homecoming game! Ten minutes later, we all gathered on the sideline to sing the old folk song, "Goodnight, Irene"— a long-held tradition to sing whenever we won. But, it had been ages since the last home victory, so several fans had to look on their programs for the words. Nevertheless, the old song sure did sound sweet that night.

Later, at the dance, I mentioned seeing a cheerleader dressed in a strange long green skirt to Satara. She looked at me as if I were crazy. She had no idea who the girl was. Then, when she leaned up and kissed me, I forgot about the other cheerleader as well. But I would never forget that night, the long runs, or the kick that won the game.

We won three more games that year. That was two more victories than Irene had tallied anytime in the past decade. For all of us, it was a season to remember. I was named second-team all-district and new player of the year. I was so enthused by what had happened in football that I went out for basketball, golf, track, and baseball (and I was lousy at all of them). I also joined the debate team, performed in our one-act play, hopped onto the yearbook staff, and made the honor roll. Oh, yes, I also helped clean up the tennis courts and became the first boy in twenty years to make it to state for Irene in tennis. What thrilled me even more than finishing sixth in the state meet was Satara won fourth the first year she played.

As the final day of school ended, I was strangely sad. I wondered how I could survive a boring summer without school. What I didn't know was my grandfather had a surprise for me that would not only open up opportunities for new adventures in the future but would also unlock some mysteries from my past.

CHAPTER 17

I knew I had my work cut out for me during the summer. I was smart enough to realize my initial success in football had been as much luck as talent. In truth, I knew very little about the game and was simply not big enough or strong enough to really be a force on the field each week. I also didn't want to limit myself just to the offense—I wanted to be able to go both ways. So, I vowed to spend my summer working out.

Jake Gibson, a neighbor of my grandparents, needed a boy to help him bale hay. I took the job, not for the money, but just to get in a good six hours or more a day of hard manual labor. So, whenever the phone rang, which was quite often, Mr. Gibson was calling to tell me he had another job. During those times, I would get to spend the hot days in the fields lifting and getting uncomfortably sweaty. Yet, I knew this work alone would not be enough to get me where I wanted to be physically. So I asked Grandpa if I could clean up part of the barn and buy some weights with the money I was making. Not only did he agree, he enthusiastically pitched in to help me out.

The old barn was filled with decades of junk. Grandpa and Grandma never seemed to throw anything away—they just stacked it in the barn. One rainy day when I wasn't out in the fields with Mr. Gibson, Grandpa and I begin to clear out one corner of the old building. Within an hour, we had uncovered five chicken pens, four sawhorses, a seemingly limitless supply of boxes and jars, several rolls of old wire fencing, three crates filled with old tools, and a dozen ancient tires. I made use of those. I laid them out beside the barn two by two to use in footwork drills.

By lunch, Grandpa and I had moved three truckloads of stuff from the barn to the drive and we were covered in layers of dirt. Because of our efforts, I now had a twelve-by-twelve foot area to use as my own personal training quarters. Grandpa spent the rest of the day building me a weight bench and some racks to hold the weights. Meanwhile, I loaded up the junk we had pulled out of the barn into a wagon. Grandpa and I were going to take those items to the dump later in the week.

Coach Boyd had given me a list of weight exercises to do. So, as soon as the barn was set, I went to work. For the next week, I lifted in the morning before I worked with Mr. Gibson and then again at night. I also ran three miles across the fields and did thirty sixty-yard sprints, twice a day. Yet, even with all of this working out and my job, I still had a lot of time on my hands, and there was nothing worse than being a bored teenager. I couldn't wait until August 16 when I would turn sixteen and get my driver's license. Then, I could go over and see Satara or the guys from the team any time I wanted. Until then, I made the most of the hours by getting in extra workouts in the barn.

One night when I had finished lifting, I stretched my five-foot-ten-inch frame, jumped up, and grabbed onto a rafter. I hung there for a second before opting to use the old wood beam to do some chin-ups. I was just completing my seventh when the single light hanging from the center of the old barn reflected on something to my left. Turning my head, I hung there for a moment staring at a spear of light reflecting through a hole in what looked like a dusty old tarp. I wondered why I had never noticed that tarp before. Then it dawned on me that I had never looked around the barn from this angle.

CHAPTER 18

Dropping to the floor proved this premise. I looked back at the same spot, and there was no reflection, not even a glint of anything that shined. Pushing aside an old bike, a few feed buckets, and a pig-feeding bin, I made my way to an ancient wagon that must have once hauled grain. I jumped up and climbed over a bunch of old chairs, at least one table, and a wooden desk. Finally, when I was on the far side of the wagon, I again saw the tarp, but I still couldn't tell what it was concealing.

Leaping off my perch, I jumped an old barrel and made my way to the tarp and the mystery in hiding. Except for a couple of rusted birdcages that rested on top of the tarp, there was now nothing between me and my goal. I hurriedly grabbed the cages and tossed them up with the other stuff on the wagon. Then I took a deep breath and used the dim light to study what lay in front of me. I really figured there'd be nothing of any value, but nevertheless I felt like a kid on Christmas morning.

I reached down to the barn floor and found the edge of the thick, drab-green canvas. Using all the strength I had gained through a month of weight training, I yanked up a corner. When I did, I unleashed a huge dust storm that literally clouded over what little light there was in the rickety wooden structure. For the next minute or so, I coughed so hard that I cried. The water that came out of my eyes quickly turned to mud when it met the dirt on my face. When things finally settled down and my vision cleared, I got a look at the mystery. The small part of the canvas I'd managed to pull back revealed a front fender of an old car.

Ten minutes later, still covered with dirt and sweat, I walked into the living room where my grandparents were watching television. Grandma took one look at me and almost fell out of her chair.

"What in the world happened to you?" she asked. "Did you fall into a pig sty?"

I didn't know what a pig sty was, but I knew I hadn't fallen into one. So rather than try explain how I had gotten so dirty, I just ignored her question and turned to my grandfather.

"I found a car!" I exclaimed.

He studied me for a moment, a bemused look on his face, and then shrugged. "You found a car?"

"Yes, sir," I replied. "In the barn. I was doing chin-ups on the rafter, and I spotted something shiny. I worked my way back over an old wagon and pulled up a corner of a tarp and saw it. It was some kind of old car."

Grandpa could tell I was excited though I am not sure either one of us understood exactly why. It probably had something to do with the fact I was about to get my driver's license, and like every other boy in the world, I wanted my own set of wheels. In the back of my mind, I just assumed this car was *it*. It had to be. Why else would I have found it now?

"Actually," Grandpa began, "you didn't find an old car. What you found is actually an old truck. It has been sitting there for almost twenty years."

"Really?" I replied. "It's yours?"

"Well," Grandma cut in, "not exactly ours. In truth, it's probably legally yours."

I was really confused now. But before I could ask another question and clear things up, Grandpa began to explain.

"My father bought that truck new. He ordered it from the factory, and the Ford Motor Company made it just like he wanted it. Your grandmother and I were already married when it arrived at Patterson Ford in Hillsboro. He asked us to drive him down there to pick it up. It was the very first new car he had ever bought, and he was so excited.

"Anyway, he drove that red and white 1957 Ranchero for the next twenty years. He kept it in perfect condition. He babied its 312 Thunderbird V-8 engine just like he babied his grandkids. So you couldn't believe how surprised I was when he gave the old truck to your mother when she turned sixteen. Until she graduated from college, it took her everywhere she went. When she and your dad moved to Chicago, she brought the truck back here and asked me to keep it for her. I didn't want it to deteriorate, so I put it up on blocks, drained the radiator and gas tank, put mothballs everywhere to keep out the mice and rats, and coated the body with a grease preserver used by the military to keep the rust off trucks and Jeeps during transport. Then I covered it. The truck has been waiting ever since. I guess, waiting for you. That is if you want it?"

"Do I want it?" I cried out. "Of course. Can we get it running before school?"

"We've got two months," he answered, "I bet we can. It probably needs new tires, rubber in the doors, and we'll have to redo the interior. We'll also have to take the engine apart and rebuild it. Brakes, front end, and the transmission will probably all need work, too. If that grease stuff worked, the paint should be in great shape. Glass should be good too. Yeah, I think we can get her running for you."

CHAPTER 19

I could barely sleep that night. And the next afternoon when I got in from work, the old truck greeted me in the driveway. Grandpa and Grandma had pulled it out, cleaned it up and opened the windows, letting air in for the first time in years. The hood was up, and I could see my Grandpa leaning over, pulling stuff off the engine. As I ran up to join him, he grinned. For the first time in our lives, the two of us really had something in common. Over the next two months, we would spend the hours when I wasn't working at my job or working out, working on a real labor of love. On August 16, my sixteenth birthday, the '57 fired up again. A few hours later, I was driving down the old road that ran past the farm. Though it was the hottest day of the year, I had never felt cooler! I had my wheels, I was in the best shape of my life, and it seemed that I could do anything I wanted. However, as I would soon find out, everything has a price. In this case, the cost of football seemed really high.

Football practice began a week before the first day of school. We started with two-a-days, which meant I was out of the house and into the old '57 by 5:30 in the morning in order to be suited out and on the field by 6:30. The early practices were spent mainly on conditioning drills. Even though I was in incredible shape, the two hours were brutal. We ran more sprints than I could count. At the end of each session, I could barely drag myself to the old truck and drive back home.

I usually rested until lunch and then would go out to the barn and lift weights for about an hour. The rest of the afternoon I did very little, trying to conserve what energy I had left for the afternoon practice.

At six, the seventeen of us who were out for football were back on the field. After stretching and a few sprints, we worked on fundamental drills in blocking, tackling, and passing for about a half an hour. The next hour was spent on offensive plays and defensive sets. We ended the afternoon session by climbing onto the school bus and being driven two miles into the country. The coach dropped us off, and we jogged back to the school in full pads. Then, most of the kids grabbed a shower and limped home. Jimmy and I stuck around and worked on field goals and extra points. I knocked off at 8:30—one, because I was dog tired, and two, because that was about the time Satara got out of volleyball practice. I had decided my job was to save her folks a trip to school by giving her a ride home in the Ranchero. As her house was on the way, her best friend, Mindy Jo Schenk, usually rode with us too. That was fine with me because it meant Satara had to sit in the middle of the old truck's bench seat.

By the time school started a week later, I was not only in shape, but it was pretty well understood that Satara and I were an item as well. She went to church with me each Sunday, I ate supper at her house at least once a week, and we usually caught a movie at the Texas Theater in Hillsboro on Saturday night. Coach seemed a bit concerned that my relationship with Satara might cause me to lose focus on football, but I think my work ethic in two-a-days quickly quelled his worries. As a matter a fact, I wanted so badly to be all I could be for Irene that I even joined the cross-country team. As much as we ran each day in football practice, the three-point-one miles I had to cover in a cross-country meet didn't seem like that far anyway. And while I never finished near the front in the meets, I always managed to win some points for the team. Still, what I really loved was not running over dirt trails, but running from guys trying to knock the stuffin' out of me.

CHAPTER 20

Our first game was against the Menlow Midgets. Though their name indicated their school was small-time, Menlow had long been one of the top football programs in six-man football. They were tough and had beaten us nine of the past eleven years. Last year, they had forty-fived us at halftime. Yet, we were a different team this year. I think the players and fans at Menlow sensed it as they watched us file off the bus. Though it had not been planned, each of us wore a very serious look as we climbed out that day. It was a look that no one expected from Irene. It had to be clear we were focused and determined to come out onto the field and take the game to the Midgets. In our minds, and soon in a lot of other folks', we were a new Irene; tonight was our first chance to prove it.

As was the case in many six-man games, Menlow began the night with an onside kick. This type of squib kick was employed not so much as a way to regain possession of the ball as it was to keep the opponents from having long returns. In six-man, the wide-open field made long kickoff returns a real danger.

We recovered the onside kick at our own thirty-five-yard line. I ran off tackle for seven yards on the first offensive play of the season. That began a methodical drive down the field. I scored the first touchdown of the year by carrying two of Menlow's men the last four yards. It was then I realized I was not only four inches bigger and twenty pounds heavier than last year, but I was lot stronger too. My time in the barn had really paid off.

The Midgets played tough—they hit hard, and their solid fundamentals made up for their lack of talent and speed. But ultimately, they were no match for us. The game was close for a quarter and a half, but then Jimmy intercepted a pass and returned it for a touchdown. After I had kicked the PAT, we went up 32-15. We stretched the lead in the third quarter and even played some of our young kids in the last period. The final score was Irene 64, Menlow 27.

CHAPTER 21

The next week we played our first home game. The squad from Lockridge was willing, but they could not stay with our speed. I added six touchdowns to the four I had scored during the first game, and we ended this one early. The Mercy Rule knocked the Armadillos out early in the fourth.

Now that we knew how to win and had gotten a taste of success, we practiced even harder. It paid off as each week, we won more easily.

Five games into the season, we had a perfect record, and everyone was talking district title. However, when we played our first game that really *meant* something, the wheels came off. The Leroy Lizards hit me hard the first time I carried the ball. I fumbled. Before the half, I coughed the pigskin up two more times. Jimmy also tossed two interceptions. Down 36-8 at after two quarters, the locker room was anything but a happy place. Coach Boyd yelled and screamed for five minutes, then outlined a plan for us to make a comeback in the second half. For a while, it seemed like his plan would work.

I began the third quarter by intercepting a Lizard pass and returning it for a TD. Two plays later, their running back fumbled, and Jeremy scooped it up on the bounce and ran thirty-five yards into the end zone. Suddenly it was 36-24, and we had hope. Leroy then got refocused, putting together an eight-play sixty-yard drive that ended with another touchdown. They missed the extra point kick, but still had us by eighteen points with only two minutes to go in the third quarter. It took us almost four minutes to answer with a touchdown of our own. Jimmy faked a pass then pitched it back to me. I raced toward the right sideline, then, just before getting to the line of scrimmage, stopped and heaved a pass toward the end zone. One of our freshmen, a tough little kid named Andrew Bell, made a diving catch. After my extra point kick, we felt as if we were back in the game.

Down ten, we kicked an onside kick, something we never did, because I could kick the ball out of the back of the end zone most of the time. Our squib kick caught Leroy napping. They were already leaning the wrong way when I began to approach the ball. After we had recovered that kick, we began an eight-play forty-two-yard drive to pay dirt. With 3:03 left, we were down 42-40. All we had to do was get the ball back, and we knew we could win.

This time, the onside kick didn't roll our way. Leroy got the ball on the thirty-five. Now they were forty-five yards from a touchdown that would drive the final nail in our coffin. We held them to a total of two yards on their first two plays. With just under 2:00, we called time out. If we could stop them and make them punt, then we would still have time to work our way into at least field goal position. As we waited for the official to blow his whistle and signal for the play clock to begin, a huge drop of rain hit my helmet. A Texas Blue Norther had blown in, and not more than five seconds later the sky turned loose with a downpour unlike any I had ever seen. Worse yet, the wind was gusting up to fifty miles an hour, right in our faces.

As Leroy came back to the line of scrimmage, the rain was blowing right into my eyes. I heard rather than saw the snap. A second later, I felt a huge lineman hit me right in the middle of the chest. Somewhere between the drops, I caught sight of the Lizards's tailback racing by me. Sliding across the wet grass like a snake, I finally rolled over and stopped. I got to my feet just in time to see the ball carrier cross the end line. They missed the extra point, so we still could have scored and kicked a PAT to tie the game and send it into overtime, but the wet ball was knocked out of my hands on the second play of our drive. We finished the contest watching the Lizard quarterback take a knee. While they celebrated, I walked toward the locker room, the driving rain hitting the top of my head and thankfully, concealing the tears that were streaming down my face. Though no one in the locker room blamed me, I knew my fumbles had cost us the game.

CHAPTER 22

I was the last person out of the door that night. I delayed my exit because I didn't want to have to face our disappointed fans. By the time I finally opened the door, strolled through the gym and out to the empty parking lot, the rain had stopped. Opening the door to the old '57, I slid behind the wheel and stared straight forward. A second later, a voice caused me to all but jump out of my skin.

"You played hard, Thomas," she said.

Quickly jerking to my right, I squinted, trying to make out the figure sitting beside me in the darkness.

"Don't blame yourself," she continued. "Sometimes things happen, and we just have to accept them. There will be another game, and you will get another chance."

As my eyes grew accustomed to the dim light, I recognized the cheerleader who I had first seen on the sideline during last year's Homecoming game. I knew I knew her, but even now, when she was only two feet from me, I could not put a name with her face. She appeared to be about my age, maybe a year older, but even if she were wearing a green and white cheerleader outfit, she was not in our school. I'd never seen her in the hallways or in any of my classes.

"Who are you?" I whispered. Yet before she could answer, I heard something rapping on the truck's driver's side door window. Turning to my left, I caught Satara's image through the rain-streaked glass. I quickly rolled down the window.

"Hey," she said. "How are you?"

"Look," I literally cried out. "Look, it's her!"

"Who?"

"The cheerleader!" As I replied, I jerked my head to the right and shot a glance to the passenger side of the old truck. A flash of lighting proved what Satara had evidently already seen. There was no one in the '57 with me. I was alone.

Slowly turning back to my left, I sighed, "I swear she was here."

"Who was?"

"The cheerleader in the funny outfit I first saw at Homecoming last year. She sat right here in the truck and talked to me."

"Are you sure you weren't dreaming?"

"Maybe I was," I responded, now uncertain about everything. "Maybe I got hit harder than I thought during the game. Maybe I am a little woozy or something. But she seemed so real."

CHAPTER 23

As the season rolled on, I continued to look for the mystery girl, but if she came to any more of our games, I didn't see her. I thought I caught a glimpse of her at the homecoming dance, but it was probably just some kind of weird reflection caused by the movement of the streamers we'd hung from the ceiling. And soon, as we regained our winning form, I refocused on football and tried to put the cheerleader out of my mind.

We won the rest of our district games and finished second. As the top two schools from each district went to the state playoffs, we finally got an opportunity at postseason play. We won the first two rounds fairly easily. In the second game against Bogart, I scored nine touchdowns—a Texas six-man playoff record. We beat the Falcons easily. Then, we ran into the number one-ranked team in the state, the Elsie County Shorthorns.

We built up a sixteen-point lead by half-time, but it had taken a toll on us. Our two best defensive linemen, Jinx Taylor and Rocky Esposito, had been dinged up so badly they couldn't start in the second half. James Black and Skeeter Lewis, the backup linemen, were both undersized and freshmen. The only playing time they'd gotten all year was during our blowouts. Therefore, they had never faced a really tough opponent. The Shorthorns' size and speed were simply too much for the two kids to handle. Using their big bruising fullback, Larry Taylor, Elsie County literally marched through our line at will. By the end of the third quarter, the Horns had tied the game. As we couldn't stop them, the contest became a scoring duel.

In the last quarter, the coach called my number on almost every offensive play. He wanted to burn as much time off the clock as he could by sticking to our ground game—a strategy that worked well. We scored three touchdowns and with just two minutes to play, held onto an eight-point lead, 64-56. A minute later, a fake to Taylor and a pass down the left sideline put the Shorthorns even. With fifty-eight seconds on the clock, everyone from Irene still felt pretty good. Then disaster struck on a play that was so bizarre, I didn't completely understand it until I had a chance to look at the video the next day.

Jimmy found Jeremy with a short pass over the middle. When Jeremy turned to run, he was hit by Elsie County's Taylor. Taylor's helmet punched the ball back toward the original line of scrimmage. Jimmy dove for it and managed to corral the slippery pigskin just inches off the ground. Yet, as he tried to secure it, he ran into our center, Jumbo Jones. The ball bounced off Jumbo's shoulder pads in the opposite direction. Jeremy, now back on his feet, raced toward the ball, but before he could jump on it, a Shorthorn safety, Collin Mach, yanked it out of the air and began racing down the right sideline. I was our only hope. I took a pursuit angle that should have allowed me to stop the scoring play. As I closed, I launched my body into the air and hit Mach at our twenty. When I pulled him to the ground, he somehow tossed the ball over his shoulder. We both hit the turf just as Taylor caught the lateral. Three seconds later, he struck pay dirt. A bad snap caused the Shorthorns to run the ball in rather than kicking the extra point. With just thirty seconds to go, the score stood 71-64.

Elsie County booted an onside kick to prevent a return. After Jeremy covered the kick, we got the ball at midfield,—the forty. Just as we had the year before at Homecoming, we pulled a trick from Coach's bag. This time we caught our opponents off guard. Our hook and ladder play worked to perfection. Jimmy tossed a five-yard quick slant pass to Jeremy. He caught it and pitched it back to me. I easily covered the last thirty-five yards to the end zone. Now we were only down by one.

The Shorthorns used both of the timeouts before we finally got to line up for the extra point kick. The snap was good, Jimmy's hold was solid as well. However, the ball barely got off the tee. Elsie County had decided to "sell out." Just like a fire drill, they put all their men into a full rush. No one stayed back as a safety. It was a great plan, too. If Jimmy had decided to pull up and pass to one of our open men in the end zone, all we would have done was tied the game and put it into overtime. Yet if their six-man rush worked and we did try to kick it, odds were they would get a hand on the ball. And they got more than a hand. The middle linebacker blocked the kick with his chest. The final score was 71-70. The newspapers would call it the most exciting game in six-man history. But to those of us wearing Irene green, it was the worst game ever played. The season was over!

CHAPTER 24

Christmas came and went. I was named the All-State halfback by the state's newspaper writers in their January poll. During the winter, I even made a few points for our basketball team, but the pain of losing that playoff game didn't diminish at all. After all, we were within two games and one point of doing something Irene had never accomplished in any sport—winning a state title—and we lost that chance on a freaky play, a one-in-a-million series of events. We all knew it was likely we'd never get another chance like that in our lifetimes.

Satara and I both made state in tennis that spring. I managed to win third, and she lost in the finals to a girl from, of all places, Elsie County. However, tennis was not the highlight of the spring. The annual end-of-the-year dance was incredible.

Satara and I had a great time at prom. I got to wear a tuxedo for the first time in my life, and Satara was outfitted in a dress that perfectly matched her eyes. We certainly didn't look like country hicks. I figured that even in Chicago, my date would have been the queen. After the dance that night, I gave her my class ring, making official what everyone already knew— we were going steady. But even as I kissed her goodnight, my mind was still focused on football and the chance to play in the biggest game of the year—the state championship. I felt even if the odds were against us, we would make that goal the next year.

Two weeks before the spring semester ended, Grandfather and Grandmother Hillman had me come spend the weekend with them. I used to love going to their place, but now I was a real country boy who simply wanted to spend my extra time cruising in my '57 and jamming with my friends. Over Sunday dinner, my father's parents told me how proud they were of me and how sad all my athletic talent was not being noticed in Irene. I didn't know what they meant by the latter comment. After all, I had a letter jacket full of patches that seemed to prove that everyone knew who "Touchdown Tommy" was. The countywide paper had even run two feature stories on me during the season. And the Waco newspaper had named me "Centex Six-Man Player of the Year." I felt I was getting plenty of recognition.

"Thomas," my grandfather, sensing my confusion, explained, "colleges don't recruit six-man kids to play football. They give their scholarships to kids from the big high schools that play the real game—eleven-man football. We have visited with the coaches and the administration here in Plano, and they feel you have the talent to start here next year. If you do, they are sure you can get a major college scholarship to Texas, Texas A&M, or Baylor. There would probably be some others interested as well."

"I couldn't leave Irene," I quickly cut in. "All my friends are there. I love it. And besides, they need me on the team."

"You just think about," Grandfather cut in. "You don't have to decide now. Talk it over with your other grandparents and even your coach. As long as we know in a couple of weeks, we can put things in place for you to have a senior year in the big city spotlight! Believe me, there is a huge difference in being a "Big Man" in Irene and a "Big Man" in Dallas-Fort Worth."

While Grandfather's words made sense, they also made me mad. I was now proud to be a six-man starter on the Wampus Cats, and I thought they should be too.

On Monday afternoon, still angry, I marched into Coach Boyd's office and told him what my grandfather had said.

"He's wrong, isn't he?" I demanded. "I mean, I could land a scholarship just as easily right here in Irene, couldn't I?"

Coach took a few moments to consider what I had just told him. Finally, in a low and steady voice, he answered my question. "Tommy, to the best of my knowledge, none of the big schools in Texas have given a scholarship to a six-man player in the past twenty years. Most of the kids who sign at the Division 1 universities play at big schools. There are a few lucky players each year that play at some average-sized eleven-man high schools that land a place on a college team, but those are the exceptions. While I think it's a mistake, the best players in six-man simply aren't given a chance to show their stuff at the next level here in Texas. In Nebraska and a few other states, they get their due but not here."

Coach Boyd paused, took a deep breath, and then sadly continued, "On the other hand, Plano has such a rich football history that a lot of their kids get looked at each year. With your speed and strength—after all, you're six-two and almost two hundred pounds—you could go up there and be a real star. *The Dallas Morning News* would write about you, and the local television stations would do stories on you. I hate to do this, but I have to agree with your Grandfather Hillman. The smartest thing for you to do would be to take him up on his offer."

CHAPTER 25

Over the next week, I thought about Coach's and Grandfather Hillman's words. I really did want to play college football. I really did want to take my game to the next level. But I hated the idea of leaving the farm, the school, and the kids who had transformed this city boy into a country kid. I was torn. Finally, I rationalized that my long-range future was more important than the next year of my life. The last day of classes, I gave the word to Coach Boyd that I'd be leaving. That night, after we had both attended graduation and watched a number of our friends get their diplomas, I took Satara to the Sonic Drive-In in Hillsboro to tell her the news.

"You are *what?*" she gasped after I'd finished explaining the logic in moving to the city.

"I'm moving," I explained, with sadness in my voice. "I have to. It's for the best."

"What about us?" she sighed.

"We can write, I can call you every week, and there's email. I'll still come and visit my Grandpa and Grandma every few weeks."

Satara shook her head, a tear appearing in her eye. She said nothing and neither did I. We drove back to her house in complete silence. I pulled up into her driveway, but before I could shut off the engine, she was out the door and headed to the front door. I had to sprint around the car to get to her before she got to the porch.

"Satara," I blurted out. "You mean the world to me. I wouldn't hurt you for anything. Almost everything I've been able to accomplish was because of you. You were there for when no one was."

She didn't say a word, just stared at me with her misty blue eyes. Then, in a deliberate motion that spoke volumes, she pulled my class ring off her finger. Without even glancing down, she shoved the ring into my palm. As she did, she turned and silently walked through her front door. A second later, the porch light went off, and I was left alone in the darkness.

I stomped back to the '57, slid into my seat and yanked the door closed. Not wanting to put her discard on my own finger, I just opened up my glove box door and tossed the ring in with the other trash I had stuffed in there. As the frustration of the breakup and the pain of the move hit me, I slammed the glove box door so hard it hit the latch and bounced back open. When it did, a piece of shiny paper fell out from under the dash. At that moment, I didn't take any note of it. I really didn't care. I didn't bother closing the glove box door either—just started the truck and headed home. Only after I'd pulled into the barn and opened the door did I remember the ring and the mysterious piece of paper.

Opening the driver's door caused the interior light to come on, thus illuminating the cab enough for me to find both the ring and the paper. As I picked up the latter, I realized it was a photograph—black and white and a bit faded, but I could see it was a candid shot of two girls. Holding it up next to the light, located just over the back glass, I studied the snapshot for a moment.

"It's you," I whispered as the image came into focus.

CHAPTER 26

Sticking the picture into my shirt pocket, I jumped out of the truck and raced inside. My Grandma surprised me as I charged through the living room. She usually went to bed before ten—I wondered what she was doing still up.

"Hello," she smiled as she spoke. "Did you have a nice evening?"

I didn't bother answering but rather just handed her the photograph.

"Who are these girls?" I demanded. Then, I paused and explained, "I found this picture in the truck. I think I know the one on the left."

Grandma went over to her favorite chair, switched on a lamp, and picked up her glasses from the end table. A few seconds later, she looked back at where I was standing. Using her eyes, she signaled for me to sit down on the couch across from her. After I did, she handed the picture back to me and began to speak.

"The girl on the right is Satara's mother," she began. "The other cheerleader is your mom. This must have been taken about their junior year. If you look in the background, you'll see your truck. Of course, it was hers at the time."

Studying the picture a bit more carefully, I did spot the back half of the Ranchero. I also now recognized one girl—the one who had talked to me at our games.

"Grandma," I whispered, almost too scared to say the words, "you know that cheerleader I told you about, the one I saw at a few of my games and talked to that night after we lost the first time last season?" I took a deep breath before saying what I knew sounded crazy, "It was Mom. Not the mom I knew, but the one in this picture."

Grandma stared at me and shook her head. While she didn't try to talk me out of what I believed, she didn't confirm it could be true either. She just continued to stare, her eyes seemingly looking right through me and straight into the past. Neither of us spoke at all for the next few moments—she seemed lost in thought, and I was too consumed by the image I held in my hand.

"Tommy," she finally announced, awakening me from my trance. "What's written on the back of the picture?"

I hadn't even thought to turn it over. When I did, it was as if Mom was speaking directly to me again.

At the top, she had written "Scarlett Gable and me." She obviously had written that simply to identify who was in the photo. Yet under the names she had written something that helped define the two girls' relationship.

"A real friend is the most valuable thing in the world. They listen, they understand, they care, and they are always there for you. A person without friends can never realize a dream. Friends allow you to go places you have never been and accomplish things others thought impossible. I'm so glad that my friend is here for me. With her support, I can do anything."

The words hit me hard at first, and then they literally flowed over me like a warm breeze. A few moments later, they even wrapped around me like a blanket. The anger I had felt earlier when Satara had dumped me was gone. So was my confusion about where I needed to live and go to school.

"Grandma," I finally broke the silence, "have you ever seen this picture before?"

"No, I haven't," she admitted.

"Did Mom always write on the back of her pictures?"

"No," Grandma almost laughed, "I used to beg her to write things down so she would know the people in the picture in the future, but she never did. She claimed she didn't have time. If you were to dig out her all her pictures, including the ones of you, you would find nothing written on the back at all."

I handed her the picture and let her read the words before I posed my next question.

"Is that Mom's writing?"

Grandma simply nodded.

"She didn't write those words down for herself then," I calmly explained, "she wrote them for me. She knew they would answer the questions I had on this very night."

"What do you mean, Tommy?"

"Grandma, I'm not going to move to Plano. I am going to stay right here for my senior year. I have things I need to accomplish here. I have things to prove to myself, Coach Boyd, Grandfather Hillman, and all the big colleges of the world."

"What's that?" She asked.

"I can make it big by staying in Irene. And if I do, then a lot of other kids who live in places like Irene and play six-man football might get a chance too!"

I jumped up from the couch—still clinging to the picture—and ran into the kitchen. Just as I picked up the receiver of the old wall phone, Grandma walked in.

"What are you doing Tommy? It's past midnight! You can't call anyone at this time of night."

"I'm calling Satara." I shot back. "I don't care if I wake her mother and dad, either. I have to tell her I'm staying right here and her mother is a big part of the reason. And I don't care if she thinks I am crazy, I have to tell her who the mystery cheerleader is. And I have to find out when I can give her my ring back!"

CHAPTER 27

I gave Satara my ring again the next morning. I also called Coach Boyd and my grandparents in Plano. My Grandfather tried to get me to reconsider, but I wouldn't hear him. I even told him to keep an eye on me, that this six-man player would get a scholarship and play big-time college football. He wished me success, but he again told me my dream was all but impossible.

I bought some additional weights and added more agility drills to my summer workouts. While I did some odd jobs for some of the local farmers, I didn't get a real job. I didn't have time. This summer, I was devoted to honing my body into a machine-like state. When I wasn't lifting, I was running. When I wasn't lifting or running, I was riding a bike. I tried to turn everything I did into a workout. I even ran over to Satara's house a couple of times a week, and her farm was six miles from ours.

I bought a cheap VCR with my allowance and hooked it up to the other one at our house. I edited our last season's game films into highlights of my plays. When I had a thirty-minute program of my best stuff, I duplicated more than forty tapes. I stuffed a tape, plus a letter of introduction and a résumé into each padded envelope, then mailed them to some of the nation's top colleges. I didn't exactly beg the schools to take a look at me and give a six-man kid a chance, but I tried to pique their interest. Irene's principal, Mr. Miller, as well as Coach Boyd were writing letters too. By the end of the summer, six of the college coaches I'd contacted had written me back. I sent them schedules and crossed my fingers. I convinced myself if we made it to the state title game, I had a chance.

In mid-July, Jimmy came over to work out with me. The next week, a few of the other players joined him. By August 1st, twelve of us guys spent six days a week lifting in our barn, running in our pasture, and doing chin-ups on the rafters. Grandma fed us sandwiches every day at lunch, and Grandpa ran a "bus" service for those that didn't have a ride. When we reported for two-a-days, Coach Boyd was blown away. Even Jumbo looked ripped. So, in spite of the fact we had lost two starters and five seniors from last year's squad, we immediately showed great promise.

Unlike the previous year, we were in such good shape that the two-a-days didn't really bother us. No one fell out, no one gave up, and at the end of each session, we looked as if we could work out for another hour and still have gas in our tanks. A lot of us stayed and worked out on our own time, in fact.

Coach made me the captain, and I gladly accepted the mantle of team leader. I was now six-foot-two-inches tall and weighed two hundred and five pounds. I was rock-solid, determined, and bent on proving every college coach in the state wrong about small school players. Even more importantly, I also wanted to work with my friends to do the impossible in Irene. While I was proud of my successes from the previous year, I was even prouder of the fact that I was a part of the Wampus Cat squad.

We had no problem during the first six games of the season. We were so much stronger and tougher than the other teams in those half dozen initial games that we did not allow a single touchdown. Each of the contests was ended by the "mercy rule" at half-time. And against Juniper, we scored an amazing 88 points in the first half. Who knows how many we could have gotten if the "mercy rule" hadn't ended the game. Though few city newspapers reported much about six-man football, those who did were now writing about Irene's Bad Cats. At times, we were so good it worked against us.

The problem with putting each opponent away in the first half is that our individual offensive numbers were hurt. Rolling up a lot of yards in just twenty minutes of action is difficult. But I didn't care, and I knew Jimmy and the rest of the squad didn't either. We might not have been leading the area in yards or tackles as individuals, but as a team we were on top. That fact kept us focused on the same goal—winning a state title.

The seventh game of the season was against Vaughan. The Vikings were the best team we had faced all season, but they were still no match for us. For the first time all year, we played a complete game, but we still won by forty points, 64-24. Yet, the victory was costly—Jimmy, the only quarterback I'd ever played with, broke his arm on the final play of the third quarter. Our backup, Ryan Adams, was only a freshman.

As he had all season, Ryan worked hard in practice, but it was apparent we were not as good with him in the lineup as we were with Jimmy behind center. Still, with the rest of the squad in top form, we pushed past Naples and beat Viola by thirty at Homecoming. With two games to go, we were already assured a chance at the playoffs. But that was not good enough for us. We wanted to win the district outright.

CHAPTER 28

Not only was Nelson undefeated, but the Balladeers had only been scored on four times during the whole season. They had taken the district title five years in a row, and they were not about to cede their top spot to us without a fight.

In a driving rain, we fought like two evenly matched heavyweight boxers. No one scored in the first quarter, and even with my two second-period runs for TDs, we only had an eight-point lead as we came out for the second half. While the rain let up, the hitting did not. The contest was stopped five times to attend to injured players, but no one flinched or gave an inch each time the game was restarted. With two minutes to go, I raced around the left side, followed Jumbo's lead block, cruised up the sideline and scored. I had never had a tougher thirty-three-yard run. My body was so badly bruised even the two minor hits I took during that rush to the end zone felt like knives being stuck into my legs. As a result, I didn't celebrate in the end zone—I just took a deep breath and studied the scoreboard. We were now up by twenty. Nelson would score one more time, but essentially the game ended with my final TD. Now we had only one more hill to climb to assure ourselves a perfect regular season.

The Pinto Ponies were the final team on our schedule. They had only won one game during the entire year. As sore as I was, I was thrilled to finish the regular season with an opponent that was not going to really challenge us. Three of us—Jumbo, Zane Matthews (our end), and I—only played one-quarter. We gladly watched from the sidelines as the rest of the Cats did whatever they wanted. The contest was over at the half and we won 60-0. Our perfect regular season was preserved. Coach told us to enjoy the title and not think about the state playoffs until next week. That was much easier said than done.

That night, Satara and I sat out on her front porch and talked about what we had experienced and the potential of what was just ahead. We also laughed and marveled at how much Irene had changed in just a year.

"Could we really win a state title?" she asked as we relaxed on the porch swing.

"Oh, yeah," I quickly replied. "There are two teams out there that are as good as we are, but they can be beaten. The way it is set up, we might even face Elsie County again. I'd love to finally beat those guys."

"What about the colleges?" she quizzed. "Anyone offering you a scholarship?"

Her words brought me out of the high of the season and into the reality of playing for a very small school.

"No," I admitted. "I did hear from Texas Normal, Tech, and UT, but none of them offered anything. They looked like form letters to me. I think they have ignored me because I go to a six-man school."

"So," she cut in, "does this mean that your football career will be over as soon as we play our last game?"

"No," I replied, "It just means that I'll have to prove myself all over again. If I don't get a scholarship, I'll find a school that will let me walk on. I won't give up!"

"What do you mean 'walk on?'"

"It just means they let you go out for the sport and prove yourself. They don't pay for anything. I pretty much had to do that here, so I'll do what it takes to make my dream come true next year as well. If I have to walk on, I will."

"Before football, what were your dreams?" Satara asked.

I studied the stars for a while before answering. Putting my arm around her, I pulled her close.

"Back in Chicago, I dreamed of winning the US Open in tennis. I never even thought about football. I couldn't even picture myself on a football field. But that all changed here. Not only do I dream about college football, but also the NFL. At night, I often picture myself scoring a touchdown to win a national championship or the Super Bowl. It might be stupid, but I think I can make my dreams come true. I really do. I mean, if your mother could run again, I can pretty much do anything."

I'd never admitted, much less voiced, my ultimate dreams until that moment. I figured if I had talked about the NFL to anyone but Satara, they would have laughed. Yet, I knew she'd take my dreams seriously. It then dawned on me I really didn't know what her dreams were. We always seemed to talk about me, never her. I suddenly felt very selfish.

"Satara, what do you want to do?"

"Oh, I don't know," she quietly answered as she snuggled against my side.

"Yes, you do," I replied. "We all have dreams. What are yours?

She didn't say anything for a few minutes. And I didn't force the issue. I was content just to rock back and forth and breathe the cool fall air. Plus, I knew that when she worked up the courage, she'd tell me her dream.

My waiting was finally rewarded.

"I want to play tennis," she finally admitted. "I guess I want to pick up your dream. But that's stupid, isn't it? I mean, I didn't start playing until two years ago, and even though I've gone to camps the last two summers, tennis pros don't come out of small towns. Most of the great players are already playing in big matches by now. Look at me, we have to move the buses for me to just practice."

I felt pretty good to know I was the reason her dream started.

"You won that tourney in Austin last summer," I pointed out. "I think you'll win state this spring too. Don't give up on your dream. You can get to yours even easier than I can reach mine."

I drove back home that night knowing Satara and I had taken our relationship to another level. We were no longer just kids dealing with homework and school activities, we were starting to look to the future. Yet, as I realized our dreams would probably take us in different directions, a twinge of insecurity and uncertainty hit me. I'd already lost the only other two people I'd shared my hopes and dreams with—now I worried that someday I might well lose Satara as well.

CHAPTER 29

The first two games of the playoffs were easy. We were simply too strong for our opponents. We played Star Ridge in the quarterfinal game. The Comets were not big, but they were quick. Andrew threw an interception in the first quarter, and we found ourselves down by eight two plays later. I fumbled the next series, and Star Ridge's top runner, George Jarez, broke a thirty-yard run to add to the lead. Luckily, even though we dug ourselves a hole, none of us panicked. We knew we could score, and we figured our size and strength would wear on the Comets. Still, with the halftime score 23-16, our fans were nervous, and I was feeling a little antsy myself.

On the opening drive of the third quarter, we gained our first lead. After that, we never looked back. Star Ridge scored two more times, but we added five more TDs in the second half. Once the buzzer sounded, we were one step closer to our goal. But I was intimidated by the team that stood between us and the title game.

Elsie County had proven to be our stumbling block last year. Now they were back with the same group of kids they had from the year before, plus a powerful running back who had moved into the district from California. Jake Weiss was like no six-man player I had ever seen. He had the speed of a sprinter combined with the size of a college linebacker. Not only was he fast, but he was also quick—this meant he was already at full speed when he got the handoff. No one had been able to even slow him down during the season, much less *stop* him.

The week before the game, Coach had me look at every one of Weiss's runs on video. I studied each of them time and time again. Coach was looking for play call tendencies, but, as a part of my background kicked in, I was searching for something different.

When I played tennis in the Chicago city tournaments, I would watch my next opponents before each match to find their weaknesses. I discovered each player had certain habits that tended to give away where they were going to serve. This knowledge helped me anticipate where to move to return the ball. Thus, I had an advantage. I knew I was not as strong or as fast as Weiss, so I watched Elsie County's game film, trying to find a way to predict where he was going and to get there first.

For the three days, I saw nothing that indicated a single weakness we could exploit. Then on Wednesday, something small appeared. As I watched the play over and over again, the tell now appeared so obvious I couldn't believe I had missed it. Before the snap, Weiss always quickly glanced in the direction the play was to go. He must have been momentarily studying the hole as if seeing the run in his mind before he took the ball. On plays where he was not going to carry the ball, he didn't look down the field at all. He simply walked to his spot and watched the quarterback. When I assured myself Weiss was giving away each play call, I showed Coach what I'd found. Then, as he presented the information to the team, I considered the irony of what had uncovered the weakness. Something I had used in tennis in Chicago had become a part of a six-man football game plan.

We had to travel to Stephenville to play the game. The three-hour bus ride was not the longest we'd ever made but may have been the quietest. Few of the guys said anything at all—we just stared straight ahead, already focused on our mission. We had never felt so prepared. We didn't even care that everyone considered us big underdogs.

We won the toss and recovered the Shorthorns' onside kick. We took four plays to move forty-five yards and score a touchdown. With an eight-point lead, we put our plan into action.

I kicked through the end zone, and Elsie County ran their first play from the twenty. As they broke the huddle, Weiss studied the hole his right tackle was supposed to make for him. All of us saw the running back's look, and we knew where he was going. Zane Weiss almost got there before the Shorthorns' back had a chance to move. Three more of us were there a second later—just the first of many crunching blows, and Elsie County never figured it out. We scored five more touchdowns in the first half. The Shorthorns managed just fifteen points, both off passes. Best of all, their great runner Weiss was incredibly frustrated, not having any idea why he couldn't get started. With a thirty-three point lead at the half, we felt pretty good.

In the third period, Weiss finally got loose for two long TD runs. We knew where he was going, he gave that away on both plays, but he was so strong we couldn't bring him down. But his accomplishments weren't enough. Elsie County watched us score four more times, making the final tally 80-36. The Shorthorns barely escaped having the "mercy rule" applied. Even as we listened to our fans sing "Good Night, Irene," our stunned opponents sat on the field staring at us in disbelief. I probably should have felt sorry for them, but I didn't, because winning felt so good.

CHAPTER 30

While we had to find a gimmick to beat Elsie County, we knew all we had to do to win the state title was to play solid football. The Clark River Clydesdales were good, but we matched up with them well. No one had to tell either team this game would probably be decided on who made the fewest mistakes.

Surprisingly, the state media picked up on the contest between the Clydesdales and the Wampus Cats. All the big city newspapers in San Antonio, Houston, and Dallas wrote features about the game. ESPN even sent in a crew to show how two tiny Texas towns had captured the attention of the whole Lone Star state. Though we were in print and on the television, we didn't really notice. For us, not fleeing fame, but rather a state championship had always been the goal. So, we were not going to be distracted from our practice or the game by the attention of the media.

On Thursday before the Saturday kickoff, Coach called me into his office.

"Tommy," he began. "I want to thank you. Your discipline, your working out in the barn, your running on dirt roads, your desire, and your passion was what inspired the other kids to work so hard."

I didn't let him say anything else before I cut him off.

"No, Coach, you're wrong. I was a spoiled kid with a bad attitude who came to Irene with a chip on my shoulder. I thought I was big time because I came from the big city. I thought everybody here was a hick. I thought you were behind the times. Then you all forced me to change my attitude. You forced me to take another look at my life. I thought I'd lost everything that was important when my folks died and I was forced to leave Chicago." I teared up for a second before choking out, "I did lose a lot too. I will never be able to replace my parents, but I gained something here that I'd never had before. I learned what was important and that helped make me a good person. Six-man football saved me. It taught me the lessons I needed to learn to put my whole life back in order. I owe you and this place everything—you don't owe me anything."

We left it at that. I said nothing more and Coach didn't try to go sentimental on me again.

The Friday before the game, we had a pep rally that was so huge we had to move out of the gym and onto the football field. It seemed everyone in Hill County had turned out to cheer us on. I was amazed! But this was nothing compared to the sea of green that greeted us the next day at the game.

We played for the state title in nearby Waco. They had brought in portable goal posts and relined the field at Baylor University's Floyd Casey Stadium for the contest. When it was time for the seven o'clock kickoff, there were more than twenty-five thousand people in the stands. Because of the huge crowd and the fact that ESPN was on hand to get the highlights, many were saying this would be the biggest game ever in six-man football history.

Earlier in the week, *the Waco Tribune-Herald* had run the headline "Chicago's Touchdown Tommy Leads Irene against Clark River." I was embarrassed by those words and the story. I was even worried it might cause some problems with my teammates, but no one from Irene seemed to care. What I didn't realize was the Clydesdales would use that headline as an incentive to get the city kid.

Just as we had done to Elsie County's Weiss, Clark River set their sights on me. But the Clydesdales would quickly find out there was a lot more to us that just Tommy Hillman. While I was followed everywhere I went, the other kids did pretty much what they wanted. Our freshman quarterback had grown up a lot in seven weeks. Andrew tossed four touchdown passes in the first half. Even Jumbo caught one of them. Zane also ran the ball in twice on reverses. At the break, we were ahead 48-32.

The defenses took over in the third quarter. We scored when I finally got free and raced sixty yards for a TD. They scored two touchdowns but missed one of their extra-point kicks. With us holding our nine-point lead going into the final stanza, we felt good. Yet, as often happens in football, our game turned on one play.

Andrew made a pitch to me, and I tried to follow my blockers around the left side of the line. There was simply no room. I jitterbugged for a few moments before cutting out of bounds just inside our own thirty-seven. However, the play didn't end when I stepped out of bounds. Two Clark River defenders kept coming and hit me just as I had relaxed. My left leg went two different directions at once. I felt something snap, and a sharp pain shot up my left side. The next thing I knew, I was writhing on the ground, holding onto my knee, tears filling my eyes. The Clydesdales were flagged for a late hit, but that was of little consolation to me. When they managed to get me up, I couldn't put any weight on my left leg. Obviously, with only 6:14 to go in the game, my playing time was over for the night and the season.

CHAPTER 31

Sometimes seeing a friend injured can have a negative effect on a team. That's what happened to us. Though we were really winning—in spite of the fact I wasn't having a great game—for some reason, we suddenly went flat. As I sat on the bench and watched, Andrew threw a pass that was intercepted and run back for a touchdown. They again missed the extra point, but we were now only up by three, 56-53.

When we got the ball back, Andrew calmed down and took us up the field on a long sustained drive. We were at the Clydesdale's nine with just 3:12 left on the clock, but a safety blitz not only knocked Andrew for a loss, but also caused him to drop the ball. Clark River recovered at the fifteen. A minute later, after a four-play drive that ended with a thirty-one yard burst up the middle, we were behind by three. Thankfully, during the extra point attempt, Jumbo tackled their tailback on the two.

I couldn't sit on the bench any longer. Even if I couldn't return to the game, I had to at least stand-up and support my friends. I leaned over and opened the trainer's kit. Digging under rolls of tape and three Ace bandages, I found a knee brace. I grabbed it and strapped it on over my pants and pads. I hardly noticed the pain as I stood. But when I put weight on the injured leg, I felt like someone had stabbed me with an ice pick. Rather than sinking back to the bench, I gritted my teeth and edged forward. It took a few seconds and a lot of effort, but I somehow managed to hobble over to the sideline and take my place beside our subs.

Andrew did his best to keep us in the game. He read the Clydesdale's defense from the line and called audibles. In five plays and a little more than two minutes, we had a first and fifteen on Clark River's twenty-five. We now had two timeouts and fifty-six seconds to cover that ground and win the game.

Coach pulled a trick out of our playbook and tossed a short pass to Jumbo over the middle. The big guy caught the ball and had nothing but green grass between himself and the end zone. Yet, in his excitement, he somehow managed to trip over his own huge feet, falling to the turf at the nineteen. With the clock running, we were facing second and nine.

Our freshman quarterback called a play at the line, receiving the snap with thirty-three seconds on the scoreboard. Andrew pitched to Zane on the end around. The guys in red weren't fooled this time. They caught Zane in the backfield, tossing him for a four-yard loss. We used one of our timeouts as the clock ticked under twenty.

I listened in as Coach Boyd called a quick pass to Zane in the flat. He emphasized Zane had to get inside the five, so if he didn't score, the clock would stop as the officials reset the chains for the first down. Zane ran the perfect route, and Andrew threw the perfect pass. The play was flawless until two Clydesdales hit Zane. He fell forward to the three. We had a first down and goal with just eleven seconds left in the game.

We didn't use our final timeout. Andrew simply got the team set at the line and as soon the clock started, he took the snap. He rolled to his right, looking for either Zane in the right corner of the end zone or Jumbo over the middle. Neither was open. Because he had taken the snap and had not handed off, as per six-man rules, Andrew couldn't run past the line of scrimmage. With five seconds to go, the Clark River nose guard finally caught up with our QB. He grabbed Andrew and tossed him into the ground at the eleven. By the time Zane raced up to an official and called timeout, the clock had rolled down to just two seconds.

Coach Boyd called all of our guys off the field and over the sideline. I joined them in the huddle.

"Ok," he began, "we can run the old hook and ladder."

Before he could continue, Zane cut in: "But Coach, Tommy's not in the game for the pitch back."

The coach looked at our end for a minute and then glanced my direction. I momentarily stared him right in the eye before turning to my right and barking an order out to our student trainer, Zack Jones.

"Jonesie, get me my helmet."

CHAPTER 32

"You can barely walk," the coach quickly pointed out. "You wouldn't even be able to get out of the backfield on the play."

"I know," I replied as I strapped the headgear on. "But my right leg is fine. I can still kick."

"A field goal?" Coach asked. "Will your bad leg plant well enough to allow you to get the ball off the ground?"

"It really doesn't have to," I replied. "I'll set up right at the stop where Jimmy will put it down. I can kick a ball thirty-five yards without running up and stepping into it. I was doing that in third grade during my soccer days. Zack, give me some tape. Let's roll as much as we can around the brace and make my leg stiff as a board."

Zack managed to get three rolls of white tape wrapped around my knee before the official signaled us to get back on the field. I literally hopped from the sideline to the twenty-two, the point where Jimmy would put the ball on the ground. As the rest of the squad huddled, I forced my left cleat into the grass and waited. At that point I didn't know what was worse, the pain shooting up and down the left side of my body or the sense of dread as the seconds dragged by.

As we lined up, I looked a final time at the goal post. Just over the uprights, I could see the scoreboard. Clark River 56—Irene 53. A four-point field goal would make us the winner. A miss would crush our dream.

Funny what you observe when so much is on the line. Up until we got set for the snap, I felt a pretty steady breeze blowing in my face. It had probably been blowing all day, but until now it hadn't mattered, so I hadn't noticed. I also hadn't really thought about the fact that ESPN was there until I saw one of their cameras trained on me. They were going to replay this on *Sportscenter*. That meant if I missed, millions of folks would know me as a failure. That thought was overwhelming.

A cheerleader's yell brought me back to the matter at hand. As I took another look at the goal post, I began to play out the next few seconds in my mind.

I realized by the time I kicked the ball, the clock would probably be at one. This would be the final play. There would be no second chance. Everything had to be perfect.

In my mind, I could see the snap coming back to Andrew. I could see the blockers doing their job. I could see the ball being placed and readied for my kick. Still, I couldn't seem to see what happened next. I couldn't see my kick. Suddenly, my confidence oozed out of me like air out of a popped balloon. As Jumbo leaned over the ball and the Clydesdales got ready to rush, I began to doubt that I could kick the ball the necessary thirty-two yards.

Why did I volunteer? This would not be easy even with a good leg. With a bad one this was impossible. I found myself in a panic. If I could have run, I might have taken that moment to charge off the field. Yet my busted leg was not going to let me leave the spot where I stood. At that second, I wished I was in Chicago again.

Then, just when my confidence had hit rock bottom, I heard a voice emerge from out of the roar of the twenty-five thousand standing fans. Glancing back toward our sidelines, I saw the cheerleader who always seemed to show up when I needed a boost in confidence. She was there on the sideline, her eyes filled with tears, but a giant smile assuring me that I could succeed.

"Thanks, Mom," I whispered, my resolve stronger than before, "this one's for you."

At that moment, Andrew signaled for the ball. The next few split seconds were not as perfect as they had been in my dream.

Jumbo's snap was high, causing Andrew to lift off his knee and stretch for the pigskin. Our crowd groaned as the ball slipped from his fingers and paused in the air just above his hands for a split second. Andrew somehow reached out and grabbed the hovering ball and in one motion, brought his whole body down toward the ground. As six red-clad jerseys rushed toward us, our quarterback put the football on the ground.

I can't begin to tell you how much pain I felt as I swung my good leg towards the ball. I thought I would collapse. And as my right foot finally struck the ball, I did feel my plant leg begin to buckle. But thankfully,

Zack's taping, along with the brace I'd strapped on, somehow held me upright, and as Clark River defenders leaped through the air toward me, I was able to push through my kick with at least a little bit of power.

The ball didn't explode from the ground as my kicks normally did, but rather, lifted off like a bird struggling against a stiff fall breeze. As players crashed all around me, I watched the pigskin drift toward the end zone for a second, then my leg gave way, and I collapsed in a heap on the ground. I managed to raise my head just in time to see the kick begin to lose altitude and fall toward the earth.

"It's not going to make it," I breathed as I judged its path. I was crestfallen. All the work had been for nothing—I was sure the kick was going to be short.

The clock ticked down to zero, the final buzzer went off, and the ball still hung in the air. The game would not be over until it had come down, but at that moment it felt like it never would. It was as if time had actually ceased to move. So for twenty-five thousand fans, along with twelve players and four officials on the field, the next split-second seemed to last forever— and perhaps it did.

The sky finally released its hold on the pigskin, and the ball fell almost straight down, striking in the middle of the crossbar. It then bounced five feet straight up in the air before coming down on the bar again, literally sat there for a moment, teetering forward and back, before falling over the far side. The official signaled what many in the crowd had not yet seen—good! The kick was good! We had won!

Bedlam broke loose on the press box side of the stadium as those who had been pulling for the Wampus Cats scrambled over the railings and rushed out onto the field. Jumbo was the first to get to me, yanking me off the ground and upon his shoulders. My bad leg was still sticking out, too stiff to move, but for the next few moments I felt no pain. Glancing back toward the scoreboard, I noted our tally ran up to fifty-seven. I couldn't believe it; we had actually won! In the background, I heard someone start singing "Good Night, Irene." Then, as a happy fan rushed up to congratulate me, someone hit my left leg. The pain was so bad I almost passed out. I must have screamed because Jumbo gently put me on the ground. The next thing I remember was seeing two men in white suits hovering over me. I thought I heard my mom's voice, and then everything went black.

So while the rest of the team and fans got to party, I didn't even get to go to the locker room. Within minutes of the winning kick, even before they had handed out the trophy and the individual medals, I was in an ambulance headed for the hospital. Though I knew I was injured, I couldn't have guessed just how badly my knee had been twisted. Even as one dream was being realized, I'd soon get the news that indicated another of my dreams had probably been forever dashed.

CHAPTER 33

When I arrived at the hospital, I didn't think much about my hurting my leg. I just figured the doctors would do an X-ray or an MRI, wheel me into the operating room, and fix whatever was wrong. I assumed I'd be off my feet for a few days, do a few exercises, and get to play some basketball after Christmas. On the contrary, I soon discovered that when I wrecked my knee earlier that night, I'd done a real good job. The out of bounds hit had torn practically everything that held the knee together. And by the time the doctors got done talking about the ACL, MCL, and a host of other things, I was not only confused but also overwhelmed. But the news that hit me the hardest was what I was told just before I was released a few days later.

"Tom," the doctor began, "I doubt you'll ever be able to play football again. You did a number on your knee. It is fixed now, and in six or eight months, you'll be able to do almost everything anyone your age does. But the flexibility, strength, and durability you would need to play college ball will probably never fully come back. I'd also guess you'll never have the quickness and speed you once had either."

I was mentally prepared to miss a part of basketball, but I was not ready to hear that I was never going to play competitive sports again. Though the news floored me, I refused to allow it to defeat me. In fact, I refused to even believe him.

"Oh, I'll play football again," I countered. "I know I will. Even if it takes hours and hours and months and months of therapy, I'll get back to my old self. As a matter of fact, by the time I am done, I'll be even better than new."

The doctor smiled and patted me on the back, then handed my crutches to me. As he did, he looked at my grandparents and shook his head. He obviously hadn't bought my speech. In truth, in spite of all my bravado, I hadn't either.

I didn't do much for the next six weeks. I couldn't drive a standard shift car because I needed took two good legs to operate the brake and clutch pedals, so I had to depend on other folks to haul me around. Satara served as my main taxi driver. She also tried to keep my spirits up. Yet, when my brace came off and my leg was bent and stiff, my shaky confidence quickly turned to real doubt. I began to wonder if I'd be able to get over this injury. After several weeks of therapy and little gain in strength, I began to admit to myself the doctor was probably right. Even pushing on the brake pedal of the Ranchero hurt.

Christmas came and went. The second semester of my senior year began, and for the first time since I was a freshman, I was again detached from the other kids. Because I wasn't involved in things, because I wasn't making an impact, I felt like little more than a fifth wheel. And because my knee didn't seem to be getting much better, my depressed state of mind began to consume my whole world. I began to act like an invalid, even expecting people to wait on me. Unfortunately, most folks, especially my grandparents, catered to my every whim. But being lazy and having servants didn't make me happy. In fact, I grew more despondent with each passing day.

To try to escape the cloud of doom that seemed to be constantly hovering over me, I spent a weekend in late February with my grandparents in Plano. Rather than help, it actually made things even worse.

"You know, Thomas," my grandfather said after a Saturday night meal, "if you'd only played your senior year at Plano, you would probably still have a chance of getting a scholarship in football."

I shook my head and barked, "I could have torn up my knee up here just like I did down there playing for Irene."

"I know that," Grandfather replied, "but there would probably still be colleges that would take a chance on a kid like you if you came from a big school. They'd be willing to give you a scholarship and work with you on rehabbing the knee. However, *no one* is going to take that kind of chance on a kid who played six-man football for a town that isn't even on most of the state maps."

I didn't reply. I figured he might just be right this time. If I had played for Plano and had the kind of year I had at Irene, then some colleges probably would still be after me. In that way, staying with Grandpa and Grandma Singleton had, at the very least, cost me a chance at my dream. Nonetheless, I was still not going to admit that fact to Grandfather Hillman or anyone else. So rather than dwell on it, I changed the subject.

CHAPTER 34

When I returned to Irene the next day, I tried to put thoughts of football completely out of my head. I even cut back on my exercises and focused more on my schoolwork and watching others play sports. In the spring, Satara's love of tennis and her success in school matches allowed me to almost forget my own problems. I coached her, worked on her techniques, tried to show her how to scout her opponents, and demanded she practice every spare moment she could find. I pushed her as hard as I had pushed myself the summer before. There must have been times she hated me, but she never quit. Her effort and hard work led to her doing something no one had ever accomplished at Irene__she won an individual state title. In less than six months, Irene scored two state championships. While we might not have been on the old state maps, if we could keep this kind of success going, we would probably be on the new ones.

The Saturday night after Satara won her title, we sat out on her porch. I thought we would simply reflect on her victory and come up with a special way to celebrate—instead she turned the conversation around to my future.

"Well, how is your rehab going?" she demanded.

"I can walk without a limp and run fast enough to get to the front of the lunch line," I explained with a grin. "So I guess my leg is about as good as it's going to get. Don't worry, I'll be able to fill your dance card at prom too."

"I'm not worried about prom," she answered. "But I am worried about you. What are you going to do next year?"

"Well," I laughed, "while you'll be playing tennis for TCU, I'll be going to the local junior college. Guess I'll find a job in Hillsboro too. In a couple of years, I'll get to a four-year school and get a degree in something—I don't know what. But I don't really need to know that now anyway."

"So you're not going to try to play football anywhere?"

I shook my head as I answered, "Nobody would want me now. I mean, the knee is just too torn up. When you consider all the fun I had this year and what we accomplished, though, you don't have to feel sorry for me."

"I don't feel sorry for you, Tommy," Satara shot back, anger and frustration dripping from her words. "But I am disappointed in you."

"What do you mean?" I demanded.

"You're giving up," Satara's voice was doleful. "I didn't think you would give up on your dream that easily. I mean, you were the one who wanted to open the doors for six-man kids. You were the one who was going to prove everyone wrong."

"Yeah, but my knee pretty much shut the door on those plans."

"No, it didn't," Satara snapped, "it's your attitude and your heart that shut the door. The knee gave you an easy out. Now you can go through life saying 'If I hadn't been hurt, I would have been a star.' That's a real cop-out. You overcame longer odds making it in Irene, working through your parents' deaths, learning how to get along with other kids, and having them accept you as a part of the team. There were a hundred times you could have quit and didn't. But now you are. You haven't really tried to prove the doctors wrong. All you've done is give up." She shook her head and added, "So, in *that* way you've proven them all right. You're not the same kid who kicked the field goal to win the state title game. You're not the same guy who always believed you could do anything. You're definitely not the same champion who changed the losing attitude of the football team to a winning one. Now you are just like all the other kids from small schools who have given in to the old ideas that being from something small means that you can never do anything big!"

I didn't try to argue with her. How could I? She was right. In truth, I was as disappointed in myself as Satara was.

CHAPTER 35

When I drove home that night, I marched up the stairs to my room and laid down on my bed. My eyes were drawn to posters I had hung on my walls. There was one of the great Chicago Bear running back Walter Payton, another of Houston's Hall of Famer Earl Campbell, and a third that showed the Lions' Barry Sanders running for a touchdown. As I stared at those pictures, I could have sworn I heard those men talking to me.

"Hey, I came back from knee surgery."

"We all had to overcome things."

"Do you think making it in college and the NFL was easy?"

"I thought you wanted to be like us. Why did you quit? We didn't."

I rolled over and covered my head with the pillow, but that didn't make any difference. I could still hear their voices. They wouldn't leave me alone. Finally, just when I thought I was going to go mad, I dashed out of my room, through the house, and out to the barn. Flipping on the light switch, I walked over and sat down on my old weight bench.

"We've missed you," a voice from somewhere announced.

I quickly glanced around the barn, just to discover I was all alone.

"We've been waiting for you," another voice shouted. "We're ready to help you get back in shape."

Right then I realized the voices weren't coming from inside the barn but from inside my head. They had to be. After all, when was the last time free weights and football posters actually talked?

Out of habit, I lay down, grabbed the weighted bar from its perch and did a half dozen bench presses. I then hooked the weights up to the part of the setup that worked my legs and began a series of exercises. They were pretty easy with my right leg, but I could barely lift the weight with the leg that had been injured. Still, unlike all the other times in the past few months, I didn't give up. I kept working, not only that night, but the next, and the one after that. Two weeks later, after I had shown a bit of an improvement, I informed Satara my dream was in fact still alive. From that point on, she was over each day after school pushing me the way I had recently pushed her during her tennis practices and the same way my mother had pushed hers a generation before.

By the middle of May, I was starting to feel pretty strong. I hadn't regained all my old speed, but I was getting a little faster each day. My agility was coming back too. On a Thursday afternoon, I was thirty minutes into my work out when Satara walked in.

"Hi. How's it going?"

I looked up, smiled and answered, "Not too bad."

She walked over to the bench and handed me an envelope. "Your grandma gave this to me when I drove up. She said it came in the mail today."

I sat up and looked at the letter. The return address indicated the missive was from the football department at Texas Normal University.

"What do you think it is?" Satara asked.

"Don't know," I answered as I ripped the envelope open. I quickly read the first few lines as Satara looked on. When I didn't volunteer any information, she tried to read the words by peering over my shoulder.

"Hey," I cut in, "that's not polite."

"Well," she answered, "I have to know what this is all about. Don't you dare shut me out after all the time I've spent in this smelly old barn."

"Ok," I replied, "Coach Battles at TNU is offering me a full ride if I'll come and be a trainer for the Jackalopes."

"Wow, a full ride!"

"He wrote that while my knee injury had messed up my plans for football, he'd heard how hard I had been working to rehab. He felt my work ethic would be a valuable asset to the program."

"That's great," Satara smiled.

"Well," I admitted, "it's cool, but I wouldn't be playing football. I'd only be working with the team. You know, taping ankles, getting water and stuff."

"That's better than nothing," she interjected, "and besides, maybe you can use their equipment, fully rehab your knee, and get a chance to prove yourself down the road."

"I doubt that," I replied, "but getting a free education would sure ease the stress on my grandparents. I wonder how he found out how hard I'd been working?"

Satara didn't answer, just shrugged her shoulders. Nevertheless, I was pleased that at least a little bit of my dream had been realized. A six-man kid was getting a scholarship to a big-time football program, even if he wasn't going to get to actually play.

Prom came and went, as did graduation. I got a job working in a clothing store in Hillsboro during the summer and continued my physical therapy. This time, except for the few days when Satara didn't have to be at her job, I was working out by myself. The task was much harder than last year when the whole football team was with me each day. Still, for reasons I didn't fully understand, I kept pushing, and each day, I grew a little stronger.

CHAPTER 36

I was to report to Texas Normal on August 7. The day came sooner than I could believe. On my last evening at home, Satara and I went to a movie. That night, as we said our goodbyes, she gave my class ring and letter jacket back to me. I tried to get her to keep them, but she wouldn't.

"No ties," she explained. "We both have to start fresh. Just like when you left Chicago, there can't be anything holding us back."

I knew we both were moving into new lives, with new friends and new opportunities. And she was right when she said we needed to make our starts fresh. Still, while she promised to email me every day and accepted my proposal of us getting together for Irene's Homecoming, I was still hurt. After all, I couldn't conceive of life without my high school sweetheart.

That night, I returned home with a sense of dread. I had hated coming to Irene four years ago, but now I did not want to leave. I wondered if I could make it at TNU. The school seemed so large, and I didn't know anyone there. A big part of me now wanted to turn down my scholarship and stay home.

"Tommy," my grandmother's voice called from downstairs.

"Yes, Grandma," I answered.

"Can you come down here for a moment?"

Anxious to get away from all my doubts and fears, I bounded down the steps to the living room. Grandma met me in the middle of the room and handed me an old green book.

"This was your mother's senior yearbook," she explained. "I found it while I was cleaning out the attic today. I thought you might want to see it."

I thanked her, moved to the table and sat down. I leafed through the pages one at a time. Mom's picture was everywhere. She was an officer in almost every organization and had been crowned the queen of both prom and homecoming. After I had studied the pages of pictures, I began to read the messages that had been written by her fellow students. Obvious to me as I read those personal notes was that she was not only a dynamic presence in organizations and the classrooms, but was also very popular.

On the book's final page, I recognized Mom's own handwriting. My eyes immediately latched onto her words, and I carefully read each line.

"I leave Irene to attend Texas Normal in order find my place in the world. Yet, I feel my days here at this school are not over. I still feel there is something I need to do or someone I need to touch. Others may think I am crazy, but I feel my destiny will bring me back here again, and at least a part of my spirit will never leave this school."

Even though she couldn't have known, Mom must have been writing about me. I must have been the someone she needed to touch. And she had. She had helped me through each of my struggles at Irene. Even now, as I was wondering if I could make it at college, she was encouraging me again. She had gone to TNU, and she had found Dad there. I was now convinced a part of her was waiting for me at Texas Normal, so I was not going to be alone. As I closed the book, I suddenly felt very happy and relieved. I again had a strong sense of confidence. Coming to Irene had served its purpose, now it was time to move on.

"Yes," I whispered, "I am going to TNU, and no matter what anyone says, I'm going to live my dream."

CHAPTER 37

There were more than forty-four thousand students at Texas Normal University when I first set foot on its huge, tree-covered campus in Independence, Texas. To say that I felt lost would have been an understatement. I was overwhelmed by the size of the campus and student body. Yet, having already been given my own place as a trainer in the athletic department, at least I had something a lot of students didn't—an anchor. From the time I walked into the Bensen Stadium locker room, I felt both wanted and at home. Coach Battles made sure of that.

James Battles, a former college center at UT, was a trailblazer. He was the first African-American coach at Texas Normal and had been the school's head coach two decades. For the past ten years, the big man's teams had averaged nine wins a season. While that record made him one of the nation's most successful coaches, a couple of things had eluded the sixty-year-old. The first—Texas State had never finished higher than second place in the Big Plains Conference. The second—the team had never played for a national championship. His failure to accomplish these two things was what both haunted and drove the coach. They were also the reason some of the school's alumni were always trying to force Battles to retire or move to another campus position.

From our first meeting, when he told me my duties and welcomed me to school, I liked Coach Battles. I could tell he was a fair man who seemed to care a great deal more about his players than he did his record. As he had with me, he was willing to give his kids a chance to perform. During my freshman year alone, I would see him forgive players' mistakes time and time again, as long as those young men were working as hard as they could on every play in practices and the games. He was a teacher, a father figure, and a friend. Most of us needed all those things too.

As I grew used to my job, an irony hit me. This was the same position Coach Boyd had offered me at Bynum. Back then I'd opted to play, and now I realized that was a wise choice. Being a trainer was tough work. I had to get to practice before the players and didn't get to go to my dorm room until long after the football team had left the locker room. I not only taped ankles and filled water bottles, but also washed clothes, cleaned up the equipment, locker, and weight rooms, ran errands, duplicated playbooks, and mixed up sports drinks, along with a long list of other duties. Needless to say, during the season, I had a whirlwind of responsibilities that constantly yanked me from place to place. I was often so busy I didn't even get a chance to watch much of the games. Yet, even as occupied as I was, there was something about being on the sidelines in front of eighty thousand screaming fans that gave me a rush each Saturday. Maybe that was why I always paused several times to look up at the crowd and soak in the atmosphere.

When I wasn't working at the stadium or with the team on a road game, I was usually either in class or at study hall. In truth, my time was so limited I rarely even had time to answer my emails. I guess that's the main reason Satara and I grew apart—and why I lost track of almost everything in Irene. Because we were on the road playing in Colorado, I didn't even get to go back to my high school's homecoming.

Thanks in part to the free tutoring I received by being on scholarship, my grades came out really well my first year at school. Additionally, between the kids I met who worked with me as trainers as well as the athletes and students I grew to know in my classes, I gained a really large group of good friends. But my most treasured moments were not on the field with the team or spending time with friends in class. The times I most relished were late at night when I could come back to the training room and work out all by myself.

Strange. Even if I wasn't ever going to play football again, I still felt the need to make myself stronger. I desperately wanted to regain all my strength. I didn't want people to look at my leg and feel sorry for me. I wanted them to challenge me to a race and watch me fly by them. As I honed my body through weightlifting, swimming, and running, a new dream began to creep into my mind. I began to wonder if I could succeed as a kicker.

CHAPTER 38

During the spring practices in the second semester of my freshman year, I started to get to the field early, sneak out, and practice kicking field goals. Much to my surprise, I discovered I could now kick the ball farther than I had ever been able to high school. Though I didn't tell Coach Battles about my private workouts, I vowed to spend the summer doing very little but working on my kicking.

TNU had gone 10-4 during my first year there. Coach Battles was more than satisfied. The team had been very young, and we only lost four starters to graduation. The Jackalopes also had a great year recruiting high school kids. With all this, things looked very bright for the purple and gold in the near future. Everyone was excited. While the coach and his staff prepared to make the next year the one that put Texas Normal among the very best in the nation, I went back to Irene to live on the farm.

I was looking forward to getting back to my grandparents'. I was especially anxious to reconnect with my old friends. Unfortunately, Satara had stayed in Fort Worth to work on her tennis game, and most of my other old classmates had full-time summer jobs that kept them far too busy to play around. So, rather than be completely bored, I spent hours each day running, lifting weights, and kicking. One afternoon, I was working on field goals at the old high school field when Coach Boyd came by the school.

"Looking good, kid," he cracked as he walked onto the grass.

"Thanks," I answered while wiping the sweat from my brow.

"You going to try out as a kicker at TNU?" he asked.

"I don't know," I shrugged. "We already have two guys on scholarship that kick for us. I'm really working out just to work out."

"Well," my old coach pointed out, "you look like you're in great shape. No fat on your body at all."

I grinned in thanks, repositioned the football on the tee and kicked. The ball sailed forty-five yards and split the uprights, landing a good ten yards on the far side of the goal post.

"If I were you," Coach Boyd observed, "I might let Coach Battles know about your leg. I think you could give those other kickers a run for their money."

While Coach Boyd's encouragement inspired me, it didn't give me enough confidence to actually talk to Coach Battles. When I reported back to TNU, I kept my spot as a trainer, watched from the sidelines, and did my kicking, running, and weightlifting when no one else was watching. I also secretly studied the playbook, learning every defensive and offensive play we ran backward and forwards. I justified the time I was spending on the workouts and studying the game of football as a part of my education. By this time, I'd decided to become a high school teacher and coach. When they found out my decision, my grandparents were thrilled I had actually decided what I wanted to do with my life. I have to admit, it gave me a settled feeling as well. Still, the future was a few years away, and in the present I had a job with a team that was looking pretty good.

CHAPTER 39

We went into the fall campaign expected to challenge for the conference title. The Big Plains' other top team was Arkansas A & I. The previous year, A & I finished third in the final national polls. As a heavily laden senior squad, the Hilltoppers had speed, size, and experience. Meanwhile, we were still young and a bit raw.

TNU cruised through our first six games, winning each by at least a touchdown. As it worked out, our homecoming game was against another team with a perfect record—Kansas Southern.

Joe Perez had been an all-American kicker the year before, and he had hit all but one of his field goals for us this year. I really liked Joe. The short, stocky senior was smart, disciplined, and a team leader. On Thursday of Homecoming week, Joe was simply working on his kicking game, doing the very same drills he did each day when something strange happened. On his fifth kick, a short practice field goal of just twenty-five yards, something popped inside his right leg, and he collapsed. He was screaming as we carried him off the field. I found out later he had somehow broken a femur bone.

With Joe out, Hector Chivas took over as TNU's kickoff specialist and field goal kicker. Hector was a sophomore who had been all-state in high school. He was more than prepared to fill in for Joe. In fact, he was so good that even though we had just lost an all-American, our squad had complete confidence in the 5' 8" dynamo.

Against Kansas Southern, Hector performed perfectly. His kickoffs constantly flew into the end zone, his four extra points were true, and his three second-half field goals, the last one forty-six yards, saved the game for us. As well as we were playing, we felt very good going into the final five games of the year.

I was organizing the locker room the Tuesday afternoon after the KSU game when Coach Battles approached me.

"Hey, Tom," he said. "How are you doing?"

"Good, Coach," I answered. "Just getting things ready for the practice."

"Tom," the coach continued, "I seem to remember you were a kicker in high school."

"Yes, sir," I replied. "Of course, kicking in high school is not like kicking in college."

"That's right," he agreed, "but because of the mere fact you've kicked in games, and you have continued to work out in your days here at TNU, I thought you might be able to help us."

Looking up at the coach, I tried to figure out what he meant. As my heart was already pounding in my chest, I hoped what I believed he was saying was what he was really saying.

"I've watched you kicking," he explained. "I can see the field from my office. You look pretty solid. I feel very good about Hector, and he's our kicker, but I thought it might be good if you gave up training for the rest of the season and worked with the team as a backup kicker. If anything happens to Hector, we have to have someone there to bring in. So, would you like to suit up?"

"Would I!" I literally shouted.

"Well then," he replied, "get yourself a uniform. I think the number six is open. In your case, coming from Irene, a school where the team is made up of just six players, it seems appropriate."

CHAPTER 40

The next two weeks, I simply relished putting on the pads and being a part of the team. In truth, I figured that would be all I would get to do. Yet in my mind, a six-man kid was now a part of the team that was on the hunt for the national championship. Even if I didn't play a single down, I felt as if I had achieved a very important goal. I was so happy I even emailed Satara to tell her "we'd" achieved our goal.

On the first Saturday in November, we played Bradford University. In truth, the small private school had been the laughing stock of our conference for years. The only real tradition they had was losing. This day was no different. We were up 54-7 late in the fourth quarter when one of our third string defensive backs, Jerome Counces, picked off a pass and ran it back sixty-three yards for a touchdown. As our crowd cheered, I suddenly heard someone yelling my name.

"Hillman!"

Looking up, I saw Coach Battles running down the sideline toward me.

"Yes, Coach?" I answered.

"Get in there and kick the extra point!"

Strapping down my helmet, I ran out onto a football field during an actual game for the first time in two years. In front of seventy-five thousand people, with butterflies zooming all around my stomach and a steady breeze at my back, I waited for the snap. When it came, I took two steps and knocked the pigskin through the uprights. I couldn't believe it—I had scored in a college game!

To say the least, the Jackalopes and I had a good week. We remained undefeated and climbed to number four in the national polls. The next two weeks, as I watched from the sidelines, we kept our conference and national title hopes alive by beating Brandeis and San Antonio University.

But the toughest game lay ahead. The last contest of the regular season would match us against mighty Arkansas A & I. That game would decide the conference championship *and* whether we would get a chance to play for the national title.

I was as much a fan as a player on that Saturday night. In front of a national television audience, I watched one team wearing purple and another outfitted in red slug it out. At halftime, the score was tied 14-14. After the bands had cleared the field and the teams had lined up for the kickoff, something very strange happened. Above the roar of the fans, I heard a voice calling my name.

"Thomas."

Looking behind me, up about twenty rows in the stands stood a college girl who looked to be about my age. She was dressed in our school colors, but the clothes seemed strangely out of style. When my eyes caught hers, she smiled and waved. I stared at her for a second, then turned back to watch Hector's kick off. A & I's top return man, Paul Jerkins, took the kick at the three and raced up the near sideline. A wall of Hilltopper blockers cleared the way for his return. As he crossed midfield, only one man stood between Jerkins and the end zone. That potential tackler was our kicker. Hector avoided the last Arkansas blocker and somehow grabbed Jerkins around the ankles. As both men fell to the ground, a sigh of relief went up from our fans. But, when Hector didn't get up, that sigh was followed by a gasp. As our doctors and training staff bent over our kicker, I turned to look back up in the stands. The pretty girl who had called my name was no longer there.

Word filtered back to the sideline that Hector had torn up his knee. Even as I watched a motorized cart take him off the field, the obvious did not hit me. Only when A. & I. scored and I watched them line up for the extra point did I realize I was now the TNU kicker. Grabbing a ball, I raced over behind the bench and began to warm up.

My first chance to put a foot on the ball happened late in the third quarter. We scored on a seventy-seven-yard, eleven-play drive. That made the score 21-20, with us down by a single point. With so much on the line, my heart was literally beating a hole in my chest as I ran out onto the field to try the point after. The snap was good, the hold perfect, and—even though I didn't think I hit it solidly and the ball wobbled off the ground—the kick was good. That made me feel immeasurably better.

Early in the final quarter, we scored again on a fumble return for a touchdown. My kick was true, and we found ourselves up by seven.

Our defense stopped the powerful Arkansas A. & I. drive on our own twenty-two. The Hilltoppers then kicked a field goal to make the score 28-24. With four minutes left in the game, things seemed well in hand. All we had to do was move the ball, make three first downs and run out the clock. Yet a muffed exchange between our quarterback and center messed everything up. The Hilltoppers recovered and three plays later scored a touchdown. When the guys in red made the extra point kick, we found ourselves down 31-28.

Steven Kerms ran the kickoff back to the thirty-five. With under two minutes to go, Josh Walen, our quarterback, led a drive that took us down to thirty-two. On fourth down, we used our last timeout. There were just four seconds left in the game. Coach Battles signaled me over and stated the obvious.

"We have to get this field goal to put the game into overtime."

A few seconds later, I found myself out on the playing surface looking at those tall yellow posts that now seemed so small and far away. Right then, I heard the voice I had heard before Hector got hurt.

"You can do it, Thomas."

I looked up and could not see the girl, but this time I knew who she was. I just nodded. The snap was perfect, the hold picture book, and my kick cleared the goal post by at least ten yards. We were going to overtime!

The 31-31 didn't hold up for long in OT. In college, an overtime period gives each team the ball on offense at the twenty-five once. If both teams score a TD and an extra point, both score field goals or neither team scores, then the game goes to another overtime. The record for the most OTs to decide a game happened in 2001 when Arkansas beat Mississippi in eight overtimes.

We matched A & I touchdown for touchdown in the first two OTs. In the third one, they got the ball first and drove to our six. We held them on third down and forced them to kick a short field goal. Now, with the score 48-45, all we had to do was score a TD, and the game and conference championship was ours.

CHAPTER 41

Our offense was tired. The game was now over four hours old, and they had been beaten up all day by A & I's huge defense. On the first play from center, Josh's pass was knocked down at the line of scrimmage. We tried a draw on second down. LaSha Rogers, our tailback, was trapped six yards deep in our backfield. Now it was third and sixteen from the thirty-one. If we didn't make any yardage, I was going to have to boot a forty-eight-yard field goal just to send the game into another extra period.

Josh took the snap and faded back. The Hilltoppers had called a blind side blitz, and Josh never saw their cornerback. He hit our QB at the forty-yard line and knocked the ball loose. For a second it looked like A & I would recover, but somehow Leroy Dale, a three-hundred and twenty-pound right tackle, managed to fall on the ball and give us one more down. As the officials set the ball at the new line of scrimmage, the forty-two-yard line, Josh called time out and ran over to talk to Coach Battles.

Fourth and twenty-seven is never an easy down, especially with the whole game on the line. To our fans, those eighty-one feet looked like miles. Making matters worse, our position appeared so dire that Arkansas A & I's band and cheerleaders were already celebrating.

"Hillman!" Coach Battles barked.

"Yes, sir!" I answered as I ran the five yards to his side.

"Can you kick a sixty-yard field goal?" the coach asked.

"I've done it in practice," I replied, trying to sound a lot more confident than I really was. "I figure I can hit it now."

"Good," the coach said with a grin. "This one is not sixty, it is only fifty-nine, so it should be a piece of cake."

I knew Coach was just trying to loosen us up—he was well aware this was a long shot at best, but his joke did give me a degree of confidence. I had about a five-mile-an-hour wind at my back, and I figured if I concentrated, I could get it far enough. I just hoped I would hit the ball true and not hook it.

A & I was shocked when we came out in a field-goal formation. They were so unprepared, they used their only timeout of the overtime period to get the right personnel on the field. A minute later, the whistle blew, and the play clock started.

Matt Evans had made a lot of snaps during the game. I could tell, as he bent over the ball, our big center was tired. Still, I was not worried about him. I figured he had practiced this play so much he could do it exhausted and in his sleep. I knew Josh was just as sure that the snap would be good. Though he kept telling me I could make this one with no sweat, I realized he was much more concerned about the kicker who used to be a trainer than he was his exhausted center.

Josh gave Matt the signal, and two seconds later the ball left the ground. The problem was it didn't come anywhere near our holder. For a moment, I stood as still as a statue while Josh jumped into the air and tried to knock down the errant center toss. He failed and the ball flew over his head and didn't hit the turf for another six yards. As the Arkansas defense charged toward us, Josh yelled "Fire!" That meant we had a muffed snap and we were going to have to make the most we could of the play. Our two ends immediately went out into pass patterns, while the rest of the team turned and tried to figure out what had happened.

Seeing that Josh had no chance to recover the ball, I suddenly awoke and made a mad dash toward the pigskin. I managed to pluck the ball off the grass just before an A & I tackle made a drive to recover it. Putting the ball under my right arm, I turned back toward our goal line. As I was now on my own forty, the end zone looked like it was in another time zone.

Three Hilltoppers linemen were rushing toward me as I picked up speed. The trio of mammoth muscles underestimated my quickness. I left them grabbing air, but I knew there was no way I was going to avoid the cornerback who was coming up fast on my left. I watched out of the corner of my eye as the red-clad warrior got closer. Then, all at once, he was lying on the ground. He had been pancaked by the very person who had started this fire drill—our center.

I was now back across midfield and running at top speed. I made a cut toward the middle to avoid another A & I defender and to pick up three of my teammates, who had gotten up off the turf and were laying out blocks for me. I felt one man bounce off my hip at the thirty and then I saw nothing but green. Glancing over my shoulder, I noted #44, J.D. Younce, the Hilltoppers' all-American free safety. He was supposedly the fastest man on the field and he was just two yards behind me. I never looked back again, but instead just put myself into another gear and headed toward the goal line. I didn't stop running until I had cleared the end zone and was racing up the tunnel toward the locker room. Because of this, I never saw the scoreboard change to 51-48, and I didn't know I had left Younce in my wake. By the time I ran back down the tunnel, our fans had raced onto the field and were tearing down the goal posts. After I had celebrated with them, I spent an hour speaking with members of the press. Talk about the thrill of a lifetime!

We ended the season playing for the national title against Rocky Mountain University. I was back to my kicking chores but didn't get much of chance to get on the field. The Goats kept us at bay with a dominating defense. We only scored once and lost a chance at number one by a final score of 21-7. Still, TNU had finally won a conference title, so we had met one of our preseason goals.

As I was cleaning out my locker a week later, Coach Battles approached me and asked me to come into his office. For a few awkward minutes, I sat in front of his desk as he looked through his notes.

"Tom," he began, his brown eyes all but staring a hole through me. "The athletic department has cut the number of trainer scholarships we can offer. I'm afraid I won't be able to renew yours this next semester."

I was shocked. I wondered how I was going to afford to pay for my education now.

"So," Coach continued, "I've decided to put you on a football scholarship instead."

At first, I said nothing. I was too shocked. Sure I had won a game for us, but Hector was a far better kicker than I was, and he was going to be fine in a few weeks. Why did I deserve this chance?

"Coach, you mean that you're willing to keep me on as a backup kicker?"

"Well," he replied, "you'll have to work on your kicking just in case anything happens to Hector again. But that run against A & I showed me something. You're as quick as anyone on our team. You're probably not big enough to take the pounding a running back takes each game, but I want you to work as a wide receiver and as a kick returner. You know, one of my old coaches once told me the best open field runners could be found playing six-man football. I'm beginning to think he was right, and for the past twenty years of head coaching, I should have been going to six-man games to find my return guys."

Coach Battles got up from his desk and shook my hand. I left his office in a daze—as if I were walking on clouds. I was now really living my dream. Next year, the official program sold at all the games was going to read that a kid from Irene, a six-man high school, had a full scholarship to play football at Texas Normal University.

CHAPTER 42

I stayed on campus over the summer and worked out with the other members of the Jackalope team. TNU had lost a number of seniors, and we would be rebuilding. We would have an inexperienced offensive and defensive line and a brand new quarterback. About the only position where we had a lot of depth was wide receiver. Ironic that the very spot I wanted to play for the Jackalopes was the one that already had the most talent. As always, I again found myself as a long shot. And, as it had in the past, that just made me work harder.

When fall practice began in early August, Coach Battles named me as one of the six guys who were in line to return punts and kickoffs. For the next two weeks, I caught hundreds of balls, ran countless miles of sprints, and did more agility drills than I could remember. All these elements of practice had a purpose. Thanks to those drills and our scrimmages, when it came time to open the season, the coach had uncovered the following facts about me—I was the slowest of the six players, and I was also the lightest. But, for reasons even he didn't fully comprehend, I also averaged the longest returns. I wondered if that statistic would overrule my lack of pure athletic ability. I think everyone else did too.

On the Thursday before the first game of the season, Coach called me into his office.

"Hillman," he began. "I've decided to start you as our return man on punts and kickoffs. There will be a lot of folks, including many on this team, who will question that decision, but I just think you can and will do the job."

Two days later, I was fielding footballs in our first game against Dakota State. I did all right. I ran two punts back ten and fifteen yards, and my three kickoff returns averaged a little more than thirty. But on the last one,

I was blindsided and fumbled the ball. I was lucky this time—one of our men recovered.

Fumbles would be what kept me in trouble for the rest of the year. I lost the ball again in our second game—this time we didn't recover. In the fourth game, I coughed it up once on a punt and another time on a kickoff return. In none of those games did I break a single return for more than thirty yards. Playing for a young team that was struggling just to move the ball, my mistakes seemed to become the focal point of the season. The press wrote about each fumble as if each was the end of the world and the cause of the loss. I began to hear some grumblings from the locker room too.

Halfway through the season, on the Thursday before Homecoming, Coach called me into his office again.

"Tom" he began. "Are you injured in any way?"

"No," I answered honestly.

"Well," he announced, as he folded his arms behind his head, "There has to be some reason for the fumbles. In truth, none of them has cost us a win. We've lost three times because we have made mistakes in every facet of the game. That's not unusual for a young team, but age should not be an excuse. We're halfway through the season, and all the players, including the freshman, now have experience. I'm leaving you in the games. I have faith in you. But you need to simply forget the past fumbles, hold onto the ball like you did in high school, and set your mind on the next game."

I appreciated the fact the coach had such faith in me. Yet as I read the *Independence Press* and heard the whispers on campus, obviously no one else did. A letter to the editor on the day of the Homecoming game even ended with, "Let's hope that Battles comes to his senses and says, 'Goodnight, Irene,' to his experiment on kickoffs and punts."

CHAPTER 43

We beat Iowa Teachers University at Homecoming. While I didn't light it up during the game, I also didn't make any fumbles. That held for the rest of the season as our young team managed to finish the year with a 7-5 record. In the final game, I even caught a sixteen-yard pass.

Spring practice saw me move up to the second team wide receiver. I also managed to hold off two challengers to secure my spot as the number one kick returner. Just like I had four years before in high school, I felt like my senior year would be my best. I also believed this team, with a year of experience under our belts, would be ready to again challenge for a Big Plains title.

I stayed on campus over the summer, running pass patterns and catching kicks. I also took four classes I needed so that I could graduate on time next spring. During one of my summer walks across campus, I caught a glimpse of the mystery girl who had cheered me on in high school and my early years of college—the first time I had seen her anywhere but at a game. Even though I ran after her both times I saw her, she always managed to disappear into a building or down a hallway before I could catch up with her. In my heart, I believed she was my mother, or at least the spirit of my mother, but in my mind I still had my doubts. After all, logic said she couldn't be.

Fall practice began with a lot fewer questions than the year before. We had our team intact. We also knew who would be starting at every position. Eli Crews had grown into a solid quarterback, and the line was now seasoned enough to give the sophomore passer some protection. Though we were only picked to finish in the middle of the conference, we thought we could take the title. I learned a long time ago that believing in something almost always paved the way for good things.

We played our first game at home in front of a huge crowd on a beautiful fall evening. New Jersey Southern kicked off to us. I fielded that kick three yards deep in the end zone, ran the ball up the middle of the field, picked up a wall of blockers, and cut to the right. I was never touched. This would be the only kickoff I would return that day, as we beat NJSU by a final score of 56-0. Still, I did return five punts for an average of twenty-one yards. I also got to catch four passes, one for a sixteen-yard touchdown.

By the third game of the season, I worked my way into the starting lineup as a flanker. In that game, I returned a punt and a kickoff for a TD, caught a sixty-three-yard pass for a score and also had a reverse for thirty-three yards. In all-purpose yards—the total yards I gained on returns, passes, and runs—I managed to crack 308 yards. It was a sign of things to come.

TNU won all twelve regular season games. We simply dominated everyone we played. I made all-Conference as a kickoff return specialist. I also made third team all-league as a wide receiver. I had attained my goals, but as I had learned back at Irene, the team was the most important. We still had one more game to win to reach our final team goal.

We played the national title game at the Sugar Bowl against the Desoto University Explorers. The men from Michigan were a good group, but we were like a squad possessed. For me, the highlight of our 42-21 victory was a fifty-seven-yard punt return. For the Jackalopes, I think the high point of the game was when Royce James, a senior walk-on who had never scored, caught a halfback option pass in the end zone. What a fitting way to end the year, winning a national title for Coach Battles while we also gave a wonderful memory to one of the hardest working kids I had ever known.

I thought my solid senior year would bring out some interest from the pro football leagues. It didn't. When they came to look at our seniors, none of the scouts showed much interest in me. I was told I was a tenth of a second too slow and about twenty pounds too light. Nevertheless, I still watched both days of the pro draft on ESPN, all the time hoping that someone would take a chance on me. I didn't care if it happened in the last round. Sadly, no one did.

CHAPTER 44

I think most college coaches would have agreed with the scouts and simply advised me to find a teaching job, but Coach Battles wasn't like most coaches. Rather than suggest I give up, he encouraged me to keep working. He even made some calls, talked with some of his friends in professional football, and got me a chance to try out with the Los Angeles Stars. I was the only player on the field that hot day in June as the pro coaches looked at me. They checked their stopwatches, threw me some passes, and watched as I fielded a few kicks. None of the men appeared all that excited, but they still decided to sign me to a free agent contract. I was thrilled. A chance, even a long shot, was all I wanted. Now, I figured, if I didn't make the Stars' roster, I could be completely satisfied using my degree as a high school teacher and coach.

Right after I graduated, I went back to Irene for a few weeks. It was good to be home. I enjoyed sleeping in my own bed at night and using my days to drive around in the '57 Ranchero looking over all my old haunts. I ran into Satara's mother at the post office. I knew Satara had won her conference title in tennis and had graduated from school with an education degree. I assumed she would be teaching or coaching somewhere this fall and would be home for the summer. I was, therefore, shocked when her mother told me my old girlfriend had landed a job working for a sporting goods company. She was a sales representative and was traveling all over the country. She was now living on the West Coast. I'm sure my disappointment in not getting to see her was obvious. Of course, if I had kept up with her, made a few calls, and sent some emails every now and again, then I'd have already known what was going on in Satara's life. I might also have been able to catch her before she left the state. Needless to say, the old kicker was now kicking himself.

In late June, when I packed to leave my grandparents' farm in Irene for pro training camp, I had the same doubts I'd had when I went off to college. I wondered if I would be able to cut it at training camp. Free agents rarely stayed around a pro football team very long. And because I wasn't drafted, I would not be getting many chances.

My first night at the Stars camp, I slept very little. The next day, the team was much too busy looking at their top picks to spend much time on the half dozen of us they signed simply to show up and try out. After a few days of getting very limited action, I began to wonder if I would even be issued a uniform and get to suit up for the first preseason game. Surprisingly, when the time came, I got my old high school and college number and watched from the sidelines in the game against Denver. I was shocked when I made the first cut, even returned a couple of punts in game two at Cleveland. As my combined yardage for both returns was just ten yards, I expected to be given my walking papers the next day. When they didn't come, I was stunned.

There were two more cuts in the next two weeks before the squad was trimmed to final status. I think I would have been in the first group if the Stars' veteran return specialist hadn't broken his wrist in the third game. Thanks to that injury, in the fourth and final exhibition contest against New Jersey, I finally got a chance to show the Los Angeles coaches what I could really do.

I fielded a fifty-yard punt at our own thirty-six and I juked to the right, causing the first man down field on coverage to miss me. I then cut up the middle, changing direction to avoid two other potential tacklers at midfield. I had clear sailing after that. With that sixty-four yard TD run, coupled with three solid kick returns, I made the team. That positioned me to be able to open my pro career in my old hometown—Chicago.

CHAPTER 45

As I got on the team bus and made my way into the stadium, I was as nervous as I'd ever been. Warming up on the fabled Soldiers' Field made my heart beat like a machine gun. Yet, as the moments ticked down before the start of the contest, I began to calm down. When we won the toss and I realized I'd get the chance to actually begin the season by returning the kickoff, I suddenly felt a rush of real confidence. I was home, I was prepared, and I was ready to fulfill what I now viewed as a destiny that began on the soccer fields only a few miles from this place. My only regret was that my folks were not here to see my dream come true and hear the PA announcer say …

"In deep formation for the Los Angeles Stars is Tommy Hillman."

I was suddenly back in the moment with more than eighty thousand fans who had crowded into Chicago's Mayer Stadium. In a split second, I'd relived my life and now I was living my dream!

I pulled down that initial spiraling kick and cut right up the middle of the field. I got behind my wall of blockers at the twenty, made a move to my left and was not touched until I had covered forty-two yards. At that point, I was sandwiched between two huge defenders. I hit the ground hard and they landed right on top of me. Both of them quickly bounced up, looked back at me for a moment and ran off. Norm Santana, one of our veterans, extended his hand and helped me to my feet. As he did, he grinned and said, "Welcome to the pros, Rookie!"

A few minutes later, I was still shaking the cobwebs out of my head when I heard someone call my name. Glancing over my shoulder, I squinted my eyes in an attempt to shield out the bright sun. Then I saw a middle-aged couple wave at me, and my heart missed a beat. This couple looked exactly like Mom and Dad had just before they died. They were even sitting in the seats my father's company purchased each year. I had once watched a game with him from those very same seats. I don't know how long I stared at them. I don't think I would have ever turned away if I hadn't heard my name being called by our special teams coach. After I answered his question, I again jerked my head back toward the stands, but now those seats were empty. I checked several more times, but the couple never came back and sat down.

My first game went well. I didn't score, but my kickoff and punt returns set up some good field positions for the team. We won too, 34-21—the perfect way to begin this new stage of my career. Yet, as I got dressed, my mind was not on my performance or the victory. I was still thinking about the couple who had called my name.

CHAPTER 46

Usually in the pro leagues, as soon as the game is over and the team is dressed, you catch a bus to the airport and return home. Tonight was different. The Stars' management had opted to let us spend the evening in Chicago and fly out the next morning. After we had won, Coach was in such a good mood he even told us we could go out on the town and enjoy everything the Windy City had to offer.

As I walked out of the stadium, intent on hailing a cab, I looked up the street to my right. In the distance, I again saw the couple I had spied in the stands during the early part of the game. They were in a parking lot about fifty yards away, waving. I waved back and started to run over to them, but I stopped in my tracks when I heard another familiar voice.

"You made it, Tommy."

Looking back to my left, I found myself staring right into Satara's big blue eyes. She was no longer the high school kid I'd known. She was mature, confident, and sophisticated. She was also jaw-dropping beautiful.

"Gosh, it's great to see you," I gushed, almost completely forgetting the couple across the parking lot.

"I was in Chicago on business," she explained, "The company gave me a ticket to the game, and I just took a chance that I might be able to catch you before you left for LA."

"You know," I replied, my eyes still locked on the most wonderful image I'd seen in years, "you're the third familiar face I've seen in the past few minutes."

"Really!" she exclaimed. "Do you have some old friends from Chicago that came to the game, or did some college chums come in from TNU? I know that no one from Irene could have made the trip."

"No," I grinned, "It's not like that."

Glancing back over my shoulder, I took another look at the couple in the parking lot. They waved again, and I thought I heard the woman say, "We love you, Thomas." Then they turned and began to walk away. A few steps later, they just seemed to disappear into thin air. I suddenly realized I would never see my mother again. Mom had finished her job—she'd encouraged me, kept me going, put me in the right places, and had now found Dad. Now was the time for her to move on.

"Who are you looking at?" Satara asked as a tear rolled down my cheek.

"My …" I started to explain but decided not to finish. I just turned my eyes back toward my old high school friend and smiled, "No one except you now."

We both stared at each other for a moment, noting the way we had changed over the past few years. Then, I gave her a hug and asked, "Would you like to have dinner with me?"

"Yeah, that'd be nice," she replied instantly.

As we walked off down the street and her hand found its way into mine, I realized I had come full circle. I'd lived my childhood dream thanks to my parents, family, and friends, and I was ready to make the next step and build on that dream as an adult. And, perhaps, the person to share my dreams was now by my side again.

"You're Tommy Hillman, aren't you?"

A kid, maybe twelve, wearing a Stars sweatshirt, was looking up at me. I stopped walking and grinned. "Yeah, I'm Tommy."

The boy grinned, "I read in the paper they call you 'Touchdown.'"

"Not today," I laughed.

"They also said," the kid continued, his eyes filled with a hopeful glow, "that you played six-man football. I'm from Nebraska—my high school plays that too. Do you think I could make the pros from a small school?"

I nodded, "It doesn't matter where dreams are born, where they are realized is what matters."

"Can I have your autograph?" the small boy asked.

"Sure," I replied, taking the program and pen he handed me.

After I had signed, I gave it back to him. He studied my signature for a moment and then posed a final question.

"If I do make it to the NFL, do you think I can land a beautiful babe like you did?"

I grinned, looked toward Satara and shook my head. Before turning and walking off, I shot back, "For that dream, you're on your own, kid."

The End

ABOUT THE AUTHOR

ACE COLLINS is the prolific author of more than 80 books including *The Stories Behind the Best-Loved Songs of Christmas, Lassie: A Dog's Life, The Color of Justice,* and *In the President's Service* for Elk Lake Publishing, Inc.

Ace and his wife, Kathy, live in Arkadelphia, Arkansas, where he happily writes, fixes up old cars, and plays his vintage Fender guitar.